PRAISE FOR HARRY MATHEWS

"Harry Mathews is the only American author I know whose utter originality does not erode his heart and his content."

—Ned Rorem

"In Mathews's inventiveness and erudition he is like Pynchon, Barth, and William Gaddis."

—Granville Hicks, *Saturday Review*

"One of the most remarkable prose stylists presently writing in English."

—*San Francisco Chronicle*

PRAISE FOR *THE JOURNALIST*

"A truly novel and seductive and funny book. Stories, dreams, loves, the elegantly shaped and the humbly unhinged—all we expect from Harry Mathews's fiction comes together as never before. This is his finest work."

—Joseph McElroy

"*The Journalist* is both a slightly surreal comedy of manners and a frightening parable on the carnivorous nature of the written word. It's Mathews's most stunning and approachable fiction so far."

—John Ashbery

PRAISE FOR *CIGARETTES*

"This book is remarkable, as involving as a nineteenth-century saga and as original as any modernist invention—a rare combination of readability and ingenuity. In *Cigarettes*, Mathews has forged his most expressive style."

—Edmund White

OTHER BOOKS BY HARRY MATHEWS

Fiction

The Conversions
Tlooth
Country Cooking and Other Stories
The Sinking of the Odradek Stadium
Cigarettes
Singular Pleasures
The American Experience
The Journalist
Sainte Catherine
The Human Country: New and Collected Stories

Poetry

The Ring: Poems 1956-1969
The Planisphere
Trial Impressions
Le Savoir des rois
Armenian Papers: Poems 1954-1984
Out of Bounds
A Mid-Season Sky: Poems 1954-1991
Alphabet Gourmand (with Paul Fournel)

Miscellanies

Selected Declarations of Dependence
The Way Home
Écrits Français

Nonfiction and Criticism

The Orchard: A Remembrance of Georges Perec
20 Lines a Day
Immeasurable Distances
Giandomenico Tiepolo
Oulipo Compendium (with Alastair Brotchie)
The Case of the Persevering Maltese: Collected Essays

Harry Mathews

My Life in CIA

A Chronicle of 1973

Dalkey Archive Press
NORMAL · LONDON

To avoid needless embarrassment, I have changed the names of several persons who appear in the course of this memoir.

First edition, 2005

Part I of this novel first appeared in *Fence*.

Library of Congress Cataloging-in-Publication Data:

Mathews, Harry, 1930–
My life in CIA : a chronicle of 1973 / Harry Mathews.— 1st Dalkey Archive ed.
p. cm.
ISBN 1-56478-392-8 (alk. paper)
1. United States. Central Intelligence Agency—Fiction. 2. Impostors and imposture—Fiction. 3. Intelligence officers—Fiction. I. Title.

PS3563.A8359M9 2005
813'.54—dc22

2004063478

Partially funded by a grant from the Illinois Arts Council, a state agency.

Dalkey Archive Press is a nonprofit organization located at Milner Library (Illinois State University) and distributed in the UK by Turnaround Publisher Services Ltd. (London).

www.dalkeyarchive.com

Printed on permanent/durable acid-free paper and bound in the United States of America.

FOR MARIE

Certainly – and I say this fearlessly and from my heart – if I had to write with such vast authority I should prefer so to write that my words should mean whatever truth anyone would find upon these matters, rather than express one true meaning so clearly as to exclude all others, though these contain no falsehoods to offend me.

– Saint Augustine,
Confessions, Book XII,
translated by F. J. Sheed

I asked Patrick if there was anything particularly useful he could pass on to me "about the CIA." "The first thing to remember is that nobody connected with the Agency calls it *the* CIA. It's plain CIA."

– page 66

I

That she was the natural child of an Orsini could not be proved or disproved; but those dark flashing eyes, that dusky complexion betrayed the Italian blood in her veins.

Paris, 1971; a bright, faintly overcast spring morning, like a swath of gauze dipped in cool buttermilk; and there she was, sheathed in provincial chic, on Rue du Bac. We spent much of our time in neighboring Alpine villages south of Grenoble. Andrée's husband practiced law in Chambéry, a two-hour drive away: he often stayed there safely through the working week.

What was she doing in Paris? No, what was *I* up to? Not my last book, what else?

A crow in silhouette stood on a roof across the street, against white sky. What else? She smiled knowingly. Seeing me turning pale: "Harry, it doesn't matter," she said, "not to me certainly." I shook my head: "Just say it."

She took my arm. Quite by chance, she'd learned I was CIA. A colleague of her husband's who worked with French counterintelligence had seen my name on a list of U.S. agents.

I'd known what she would say, and I hated hearing her say it. At 41 I still longed to be thought of as open and good, to seem wonderfully transparent (and transparently wonderful, no doubt). It hurt to be thought of as a spook. Not because by that time it had become shameful but because it was simply wrong.

I'd gone through something like this already. Many people in Paris "knew" I was gay, because for years I used to dine several times a week with my best friend, and *he* was gay. QED. I didn't disapprove of homosexuality, on the contrary; but how could people see me for whoever I was if they made such a basic mistake?

Still another source of misunderstanding was my having "independent means." This had earned me the reputation of being very rich, which I was happy not to be. (Some people even cited my unexplained wealth as proof of a CIA connection, which was nonsense: if the Agency was giving me money, it would have given me a job, too.) When my grandmother died in 1952, she left me seventy-five thousand dollars outright. For several years this generated enough income to support my family comfortably. Later, when I started invading capital, luck in what I sold kept me going. In the late '60s I made good money working on two movies in Italy, and that helped. (I'd also inherited twenty thousand dollars from my grandfather in 1959, but I'd used this to publish a literary magazine and to settle loans I'd taken out to buy my house in the Alps and an apartment in Paris.) I'd lived well, and I never spent more than ten thousand a year on current expenses. This didn't stop most people from assuming I was a millionaire.

A CIA label was more of the same, and in terms of public opinion, worse. I'd quickly learned that arguing I wasn't CIA (or gay, or very rich) was a waste of time. It just kept the likelihood alive. I was crazy to care so much; but I did.

That morning on Rue du Bac, Andrée had made official what I'd thought was only hearsay.

The first time I'd been tagged as an agent in Paris was in 1967, at a left-bank gallery opening. A writer named Michel Loriod was arguing with me. He lost his temper and suddenly shouted, "Everyone knows you're CIA. By definition your opinions are worthless." I'd been blindsided. I couldn't think of anything to say.

Loriod spoke with absolute conviction, as though he too "knew." Had this meant another counterintelligence connection? Later he worked for the French government; but then? Maybe as a paid informer? He was poor; but whenever things got really bad, he had a reliable stratagem up his sleeve. He'd approach one of his friends, a beautiful Egyptian writer connected like him to the Surrealist group; she'd pass the word to a well-known Surrealist artist; the artist would give Loriod a painting for him to sell. This must have been preferable to peddling information about the art world. He was inclined to fits of violent moral indignation, which also disqualified him as a snoop, since he wasn't clever enough to fake them.

Loriod briefly figured later in my CIA career, during what were called "the events" of May, 1968. Early that month, Niki, my ex, called me in New York: she said Paris was heading towards civil war. She'd gotten our 13-year-old son out of the country, but Laura, our daughter of 17, couldn't be budged. I had to come and look after her, right now.

Like everything in France, airports were shut. I flew to Brussels, rented a Beetle, loaded it with four 10-liter jerrycans of gas, and reached Paris the next afternoon. From my apartment on Rue de Varenne I heard explosions – only police grenades, I later learned, but they did sound like war. I called friends. I luckily caught Sarah Plimpton at home, and she said she would pick me up and give me a tour. It wasn't war, only some kind of wild civic psychodrama – a true cultural revolution while it lasted, undeniably rough but exhilarating.

The previous week a self-appointed bevy of writers had invaded Hôtel de Massa on Rue du Faubourg Saint-Jacques, an elegant property that housed the respectable Société des Gens de Lettres (the French Authors Guild). The new occupants founded a Writers Union on the ground floor. I was soon enrolled by friends and so became (pace Stephen Spender) its first English-speaking member. We didn't do much except talk, but even that helped – it kept several dozen bright-eyed intellectuals busy while students and workers made things happen.

We talked and argued about subjects like: How does the writer function as worker in a workers' society? Can commercial publishing ever be fair? Sometimes we discussed the positions we should take in the current situation, and it was then that the arguments turned venomous. The great majority of us supported the student-worker movement, but there was a small, noisy minority that followed the French Communist Party line and was dead set against it. The minority consisted of the editorial board of the review *Tel Quel* plus Paule Thévenin (she'd once been Antonin Artaud's companion); it was animated by *Tel Quel*'s director, Philippe Sollers.

Sollers had already developed his peculiar literary persona: a versatile editor; a brilliant critic; except for his fervent erotic curiosity, provocatively inconstant in his beliefs; also jealous, paranoid, and obsessed with control.

On the night of May 24, Sollers's minority walked out of the Union after a vote had left it isolated. Later, Sollers often came back alone and talked to us good-naturedly enough. One evening Maurice Roche and I joined a group at a nearby café. It included Maurice's companion, Violante do Canto, Sollers, and Jean Pierre and Marie-Odile Faye. At some point I remarked how much I regretted not having better French, since I would have liked to take up Clarisse Francillon's generous suggestion that I "look after the Union archives." Sollers looked at Maurice as if to say, "And you say he's not a spy?" (There *had* been a spy. Marie-Odile caught him phoning from a back room using terms like "R2M to 316.") Two days later Jean Pierre told me Sollers had been taking Union members on strolls round the garden and telling them that I was CIA. So I took *him* for a stroll and asked him how he could talk such rubbish. Marcelin Pleynet, the secretary of *Tel Quel* and my friend, could have set him straight. Sollers backed down. He was only repeating what he'd heard from Loriod. He promised not to mention the subject again; he kept his word.

But for three weeks I'd been caught up in the general elation, and it was painful now to think that anyone who'd shared that elation doubted my motives. Fortunately, people involved in May, 1968 didn't care much what a little-known American writer was up to. Not even Michel Loriod: he acted with such consistent good sense that I gave up resenting him.

Then May was over; and I was still disappointed and bewildered. It was a kind of bewilderment I'd first experienced three years before, many thousands of miles from Hôtel de Massa.

I MET FRED WARNER IN CAIRO IN THE AUTUMN OF 1963. HE came to a party at Lili Bellenis's apartment on El-Gezira where I was staying as a paying guest. Warner was six feet six inches tall. He had a long, lively face and an intense manner. He seemed to laugh all the time, and he had an answer to everything. He spoke in what sounded to me like a caricature of Oxford English. I couldn't stand him. I felt no differently when I saw him at lunch next day at the home of the architect Hassan Fathy near the Citadel. That was where I found out that Warner and I were going down to Luxor by the same train.

On our first day there, soon after we'd arrived, he told me he'd hired a taxi to visit the temple of Dendera and would I like to share it? I could hardly refuse, any more than I could refuse his suggestion that we dine together that evening. "We'll find a place in the old town," he said. "You must never even contemplate eating at our hotel. It is guaranteed to provide international cuisine at its very worst." I suppose that's when I started listening to him.

At dusk we walked into town. Fred led the way through a maze of streets he'd never seen before to a locals' restaurant, where I had the best grilled lamb I'd ever eaten. On our way back he stopped at a corner – he'd intercepted some signal beyond my ken. He took us down a back alley to a house where a wedding feast was in progress. We were welcomed and led inside. Fred congratulated the bride and groom in his most urbane English. The crowd around us didn't understand a word but responded gleefully. We didn't stay long. (On the way out, a black-garbed mother sitting on the steps pointedly unveiled her daughter for my inspection. The girl was fifteen years old at most, pale as ice and heartbreakingly beautiful.) As we walked to the hotel, I listened to Fred's comments on the scene we'd just left and realized that as a traveler I was a novice.

We went to Dendera next day. As Fred was entering the door of an underground temple chamber, a medium-size bat struck him square in the chest; he only grunted in surprise. We hired feluccas to go across the Nile and visit tombs, other temples, and Hassan Fathy's village of New Gurna. Finally Fred persuaded me to sail with him to Abu Simbel on the *Hapi*, a little steamer of dark wood and old-fashioned comforts. These included an experienced Greek chef and a beautiful, passionate Cairene stewardess named Mimi. (Passionate all right, but not to the point of compromising her chastity, no matter how long the kisses lasted.)

By the time we disembarked at Assuan, Fred and I were friends. I came to rely on him for information about the world – he had hands-on knowledge of how it worked. He reminded me of Christopher Tietjens in *Parade's End*: the best kind of Tory, honest, scrupulous, fascinated by everything in life – art, business, war, farming, philosophy, politics, money, natural science. Also impatient, irascible, unfair (especially to those close to him), and fond of even boring grandees. He could sink for weeks at a time into a melancholy where no one could reach him.

He worked as a diplomat most of his life. In 1960 he successfully organized the international conference that led to a temporary truce in Laos; so it was logical that his first ambassadorial posting would be to Vientiane.

That was in 1964. A year later he invited me to stay with him. I'd just finished my second novel, I had no plans, I accepted – who wouldn't have? In November, 1965 I flew to Bangkok and on to Vientiane a few hours later.

Through the plane window I saw Fred, at ramrod attention, standing in steamy sunshine on the blacktop. The temperature in the sun must have been over a hundred. Fred wore a double-breasted dark suit and tie. Behind him a limo was waiting. It took us to the Residence, where I would live off and on for eight weeks.

I'd arrived in time for the main annual Buddhist holiday, which lasted a week and centered on a fair at That Luang, a kind of pagoda built around a legendary gold-leaved Buddha. For me, it meant a round of embassy evening parties.

Laos is poor and isolated, but the American war in Vietnam had made it a diplomatic hot spot: it was semi-neutral territory for the Ho Chi Minh Trail and U.S. Air Force bombers. Vientiane embassies were staffed now by first-rank diplomats. I was evidently the only tourist in the country (druggies came much later). I had no idea of what I'd walked into.

On my first night I slept twelve hours; after that I was ready for fun. The Australian Embassy was doing the entertaining the next evening. I was introduced to the ambassador, then wandered about, glass in hand, until I found a friendly-looking group. They were all smiles at the sight of my new face. What was I doing here? Nothing, I explained, I was simply a writer who happened to be a friend of the British ambassador. "You *are* American?" I nodded, they nodded and then pointedly ignored me.

The same thing happened again that evening and the evening after that. On the third night, at the British Embassy itself, I thought I knew what might be wrong. I approached three unfamiliar guests. Smiles again, and: what was I doing here? I was an engineer, plumbing was my specialty, and I was being sent to the camps up north – apparently there were problems. "You don't say? Let's have another drink."

I'd been remiss not because I'd lied, but because I'd lied badly. First and last, unofficial agents have to supply plausible cover.

Now that I had joined the club, I became popular in diplomatic society; and that was when the French marked me down as an American agent. Aside from Fred, I had one friend in Vientiane when I arrived: a handsome young Frenchman named Gérard Lacotte. I'd met him in Paris; now he was doing his military service in a minor position at the French embassy. A good, decent man – and that was no reason not to tell his superiors that the word in Vientiane was that I was CIA. So social prattle was enough to get me on that fateful list. Intelligence services make use of whatever they can get. At least that was Fred's explanation, after I told him about meeting Andrée on Rue du Bac.

For two years I made myself sick on account of this "injustice." I told my tale over and over to anyone who would listen. Of course each time I told it, another listener started thinking that maybe I *was* CIA. The worst effect was on me. I wanted to play a part in the grand conspiracy of poetic subversion; in fact that was how I justified my life. But how could I get a hearing if people thought I was an ordinary, paid conspirator? Every time I protested my innocence I felt a bitterness as futile as jealousy itself.

I HAD ONE MORE CIA EXPERIENCE IN LAOS.

Outside Vientiane I usually traveled with Fred. This guaranteed my safety in the eyes of the American ambassador, who had made Fred promise never to expose me to the slightest danger. But when on Fred's recommendation I went off to visit the southern province of Champassak on my own, I had to stop over in Savannakhet, which was near a sort-of war zone; so special measures were necessary. A USAID employee was instructed to meet me at the airport; he and his wife would put me up for the night. I didn't look forward to my stay.

At least there was a Tulsa phone book in my bedroom, with a city map in it, and I was able to look up names of Oklahoman friends now in New York – Padgett, Brainard, Berrigan – and write them postcards about their home town. I went down to dinner. No drinks. In the town market we'd passed earlier I'd seen piles of melons, papayas, mangoes, and assorted greenery. Our meal began and ended with canned beets and canned pineapple.

I quizzed my host and a colleague who'd joined us about their work. They said they were teaching Laotian peasants how to water their crops correctly; in fact they were retired military keeping an eye on the territory. I didn't even joke about my new CIA status; they were the real thing.

At the end of dinner they briefly showed some concern for me. They had asked about my plans. I said I'd be going through northern Thailand, then Bangkok, and finally Cambodia before coming back to Laos. I was hoping to spend ten days in Angkor Wat. At this point the two men exchanged looks of genuine worry. My host at last turned to me and declared, "Harry, one day in Angkor is plenty. There's nothing there but miles and miles of ruins."

Next morning I was put on a plane to Paksé, the main town in Champassak. I had lunch, then took a bus to Paksong, a village on the edge of the Bolovens Plateau. The place had once been a fashionable refuge from the valley heat, but it was deserted now: I was alone in the once-best hotel. I'd been told about a decent restaurant run by a Frenchman who'd stayed on after independence. I looked him up, and he agreed to serve me but, he insisted, no later than 6 P.M. While we were talking, he snickered and pointed at my ankles. Half a dozen leeches were nimbly climbing up my socks.

Walking around the village, I was stopped by a young Filipino, who said there would be a party later at the local Brotherhood Clinic. I should definitely come, and be sure to bring a bottle of Scotch.

The Brotherhood Clinics were set up by the American and Filipino Junior Chambers of Commerce to supply badly-needed medical care. The Americans provided the funding, the Filipinos provided the staff. They were often helped by American airline stewardesses who volunteered as nurses' aids during their long layovers in Bangkok. The party that evening was celebrating the departure of one group of stewardesses and the arrival of the next.

When I arrived, the party was in full swing. Tables and chairs had been pushed against the walls to leave maximum room for dancing. The Filipinos had mile-long reel-to-reel tapes that played old favorites and the latest hits. The atmosphere was thrilling. Filipinos like to dance, they like to party – I suppose they like life. I fell in love with a whole country on that dance floor.

After a while, I took a break to cool off. I noticed a couple dancing – pretty stewardess, pretty young doctor; but he was drunk and she was getting annoyed; so I cut in – I cut in on *her* and asked the doctor if he'd mind joining me: I was too hot to keep moving and wanted someone to talk to. "OK, OK." That was the easy part.

We sat down. He did not ask me why I was in Laos. He told me. They all knew I was CIA. I wasn't ready for this, I was probably a little high – enough to want to argue. Of course it didn't do any good, but that only made me more stubborn. So I finally said to him that if he was a doctor, he'd had a university education; and since he spoke English so well, perhaps he'd studied English literature? He nodded. "Well then, try me. I told you I'm a writer. Ask me about writers you like. Maybe that'll convince you."

He was swaying gently back and forth, and his eyes were brightening. He was about to blow me to smithereens. He said there was only one English writer he really loved. So? A *poet.* And? A pause before the clincher: "Gerard Manley Hopkins."

I enjoyed a pause of my own and then whispered:

> "My aspens dear, whose airy cages quelled,
> Quelled or quenched in leaves the leaping sun,
> All felled, felled, are all felled . . ."

and on to the end of "Binsey Poplars"; then "The world is charged with the grandeur of God . . . ," and after that (I was pulling up verses I hadn't even memorized) "The Windhover."

The doctor readily acknowledged defeat. In fact he was delighted. He nodded his head in time to my recitations and corrected me once or twice: "'Oh, morning at the cold brink eastward . . .'" – "I believe the brink is brown." We spent another twenty minutes discussing "The Wreck of the Deutschland." Finally he excused himself.

"Harry, Harry, how can I ever thank you? But now I must go to bed. It has been a joy to meet you."

"My pleasure!"

"It is wonderful to find someone to talk to about Hopkins."

"But you know so much more about him . . ."

"No – and another thing I must tell you."

"What's that?"

"How glad I am that CIA is training its men so well."

II

"TO TELL THE TRUTH, WHAT I CANNOT UNDERSTAND ," MARIE-Claude de Brunhoff was saying, "is your missing the obvious solution." She had a husky voice that told you that in her world candor and experience walked hand in hand. "Admit you're CIA. *Claim* you're CIA."

Deny being an agent, and people think you may be one. Say you're one and they'll know you aren't. A secret agent is useful only as long as he stays secret; and it was possible that "coming out" might effectively shut people up, although in France there'd always be skeptics who'd suspect a ruse.

But I was too out of touch with reality to try anything so reasonable. It had been almost two years since I'd met Andrée, and I still apprehended knowing looks like the one she'd given me on Rue du Bac. I avoided social occasions involving French people, with the exception of Georges Perec and his friends, and the Oulipo. I thought that aside from lying low, there was nothing I could do.

THERE WAS SOMETHING I COULD DO.

On New Year's Eve, 1972, Richard Carrott gave a houseparty at his house in Rochefort, an hour south of Paris. He invited a slew of clever people: Tony Holland from London, Robert Rosenblum, Norma Everson, and Diane Kelder from New York, Patrizia Cavalli from Rome.

There were also four Chilean guests. Their presence was more or less my doing. A week earlier, Maxine and I had spent Christmas Eve with two of them. Maxine, my companion for over a decade, had met Silvia Uribe in New York the year before. Also in New York, but even earlier, the composer Morton Feldman had introduced me to his colleague, Enrique Cabót. We'd each liked the one we'd met, and when we ran into them in Paris and found they'd become a couple, we adopted them at once. Enrique was dark, sibylline, and witty; Silvia a blonde heiress who loved dancing and the company of artists. (They were ten years our junior; they may well have reminded us of the passionate young couple we no longer were.) We asked Richard Carrott if we could bring them along to his houseparty; and they in turn wondered if two friends of theirs might also be included, since they'd already agreed to see the New Year in together; and Richard, who was the soul of conviviality and had plenty of room, welcomed them all.

Richard's generosity paid off. The Chileans were elegant and easygoing. The two we hadn't met were Isabellita, an actress, and Pepe, a fashion designer. Silvia and Enrique supported Salvador Allende's left-wing government; the other two despised it. The couples teased each other mercilessly when they talked politics, but even the losers laughed when a point was scored. They were like a family playing croquet, madly competitive but family first and last. With them we talked, danced, and drank the night away.

Next afternoon I was sitting alone in my Paris apartment. My living-room was full of dark-gray winter light. I felt numb and gloomy, relearning that the beginning of a year doesn't change anything. After signing the peace, America had even started bombing North Vietnam again.

Someone on the ground floor was ringing to be let in. I buzzed the door open and went out on the landing to ask who it was. Enrique and Silvia appeared on the stairs, each holding a bottle of champagne raised high. Enrique declared, "We must stay in training."

I fetched an ice bucket; we sat down around the coffee table. We were well into the first bottle when Silvia asked, "You're feeling sad, Harry?"

"Not really. Mainly post-party depression."

"And Maxine, maybe? We hadn't realized." Maxine was soon to leave Paris for good.

I said yes, of course; and it was true enough. I told them I also had publishing worries. Eventually I mentioned my CIA obsession.

"Aha," said Enrique, "you see, we didn't know you were CIA. That explains what you do with your time. We were starting to worry about you."

"It's not funny," I sniffed.

Silvia observed, "You simply have to come to Chile. I know there'll be lots going on to keep you busy."

"And more and more as the summer heats up. That's why we're going back early."

I tried to smile at their teasing, without much success. "I'm hopeless, I know, but I'm stuck with this thing. Sometimes when I wake up the first thought that comes into my head is: people think I'm CIA, they're convinced of it – people I like."

Enrique and Silvia looked at one another, then laughed.

"What's the joke?"

Silvia anwered, "It's that you have been given the makings of a glorious comedy. But you shouldn't be hanging around backstage and complaining. Step out into the lights and play it for all it's worth!"

"I don't get it."

"People think you work for the CIA," Enrique explained, "and you've learned you can't change their minds. Don't even try. Show them they're right. Make the role your very own. It's a winner. Believe me, respectable men will flatter and pursue you for information you haven't got. They may even pay you for it – and you of all people will know how to make up what they want to hear. And think of all the women who are dying to get into bed with a real spy!"

I thought: this is like Marie-Claude de Brunhoff's advice, with a creative twist. I felt I was on the point of stepping out of my well-tended darkness. We opened the second bottle of champagne. Even my pseudo-Mies chairs started to look encouraging; even my yellow boots.

"And both of you really approve of my passing for CIA? The CIA, for God's sake!"

"You could try taking the KGB route. That would be interesting. Harder, though, and riskier. Harry, it's only a game. You feel sorry for yourself because you found yourself stranded in the middle of it. But once you start leading the way, you'll have a ball.

And soon enough, whatever happens, it will all go up in smoke and you'll be out of it."

I still had doubts. "What makes you think I can bring it off? It's a whole new life for me."

"You're complaining?"

"I spend most of my time at home or with a couple of friends. What am I supposed to do – if I dare?"

"Oh, Harry, stop!" Silvia said. "Just stop holding back. You love carrying on. If you don't remember last night, I do."

"I don't remember, and please don't tell me."

"Set yourself a few simple rules," Enrique added. "Don't ever deny you're CIA. It's never worked, anyway – certainly not with us! Notice how you usually act with other people, then see what you could make look like suspicious behavior." (This had sometimes happened without my even trying.) "Maybe learn the lingo of the trade and occasionally let it show. Most important, get yourself decent cover."

This last point had always rankled. It was dimwitted to take me for CIA when every CI agent abroad had a job – at least a diplomatic post, best of all a "real" job. It was a basic requirement.

"You really think I can do it?"

"You can do it."

I thought: they're probably right. They seem to know me better than I know myself. "OK. But if things go wrong, you buy me a ticket to Santiago."

"Don't forget to send us a postcard."

And so I surrendered to this new Idea.

We went to the movies to celebrate. *The Tall Blond Man with One Black Shoe* turned out to be even funnier than we expected.

January, 1973 was a good time to start a new life. I was on my own for the first time ever. The two children I'd looked after since my marriage broke up were gone – my daughter in 1969, my son in 1972 – and now Maxine, who'd been with me for twelve years, decided she'd had enough and went back to New York. Two of my closest friends were oceans away, John Ashbery in America and Fred Warner in Japan. Georges Perec, who'd become a mainstay of my life in Paris, was so busy making his first movie that I only saw him rarely. I had several women friends who somehow managed to put up with my spasmodic dating (maybe they liked it) but none of them was a regular companion.

My writing life had almost stopped. My third novel had been going the rounds of New York publishers for four years. I wasn't about to start another one.

So my Idea had plenty of space to grow in. I'd have to drop my plan to relearn classical Greek, something that looked to me now like a pathetic exercise in sopping up spare time. The one really unpleasant consequence I faced was deliberately associating myself with an organization that in my world was universally condemned. But wasn't that a price I was paying already? Wasn't actually choosing to look bad what made this gambit exciting, what would make it work? The new game certainly seemed more promising than moping at home in front of my mirror wondering how fast I was losing my hair.

A MONTH LATER, ONE OF MY WOMEN FRIENDS GAVE ME MY FIRST real chance to play spy.

Before that I practiced. Books weren't much use, aside from a few novels, and who can trust a novelist? Other writers were mainly interested in bashing CIA, not in explaining how it worked, except for curiosities like Castro's exploding cigar. I did my best to imagine how a secret life would look. Whenever I went into a place, I'd make a point of stopping and checking it out. I always walked along the sidewalk opposite my building before crossing the street to my front door. At parties I sometimes drank nothing but mineral water – that was sure to be noticed. I decided that leading the life of a secret agent was like having an affair with a gangster's wife.

Sometimes I could make use of an ordinary situation.

I smoked cigars, preferably Havanas. In Paris these were expensive and uneven in quality; in Geneva they were reliable and reasonably priced. Geneva wasn't far from my place in the Alps, and whenever I went there I always bought as many as I dared take through French customs. The year before, I'd talked about cigars to one of the headwaiters at Lipp's, the fashionable *brasserie* at Saint Germain-des-Prés. He'd told me that Rafael Gonzales lonsdales were his favorites, and twice I'd brought him a box of twenty-five, which he paid for on the spot. I still had one box I could deliver.

For several days I staked out Lipp's from the Café de Flore across the street. At dinnertime I checked to make sure my headwaiter was on duty, then took a seat at a front table of the café.

Even when the traffic was heavy I could spot most of the people going into the *brasserie*. I waited for someone who was sure to know me.

At nine o'clock on the fourth evening Charlotte Aillaud appeared on the far sidewalk, coming from Rue du Dragon with her son Gilles and his buddy Eduardo Arroyo. Between them they knew everyone in Paris, even me. They disappeared into Lipp's. I followed them a few minutes later. I saw they'd taken their usual table front and right and stopped where I was sure they could see me. I spent a moment scanning the rest of the room with what I hoped was conspicuous discreetness, then walked straight back to where my headwaiter was standing. I slid the wrapped cigar box from under my overcoat; he tucked it under one arm, took a wallet from his breast pocket, and with a polite nod handed me several large bills. I turned and walked back out, keeping my eyes down.

Three weeks later I spent an evening at Maurice Roche and Violante's. Maurice joshed me: if I was using Lipp's as a drop, I should at least try their beer. I shrugged and asked for another Scotch. It *was* something to drink to.

All the same, slipping a headwaiter a package couldn't qualify as unambiguous evidence of intelligence activity. An opportunity to produce that kind of evidence came with an unexpected phone call from Marie-Claude Podopoulos.

I HAD BEEN GOING OUT WITH MARIE-CLAUDE, OFF AND ON, FOR a year. She was in her mid 20s, pretty, smart, thrillingly cool, still living with her parents when I met her. I often saw her father when I called for her – Eugène Podopoulos, a well-known cardiologist. (Because I knew his daughter, he personally supervised a stress test I took at the American Hospital.)

Marie-Claude was phoning me because of something "a friend" had told her. He'd been hurrying to catch a 63 bus at the Raspail stop on Boulevard Saint-Germain. He'd missed it, but he'd come close enough to see me stepping on board just before the doors closed. He waited for the next bus; and at the following stop, he was astonished to see me getting on once again. He became curious. What was I doing? Why would I change busses going in the same direction on the same route? He decided to follow me.

I'd hopped off at Carrefour de l'Odéon and walked down Rue de l'Ancienne Comédie to a gallery just past Rue de Buci. I'd entered the gallery, come out less than a minute later, and set off down Rue Dauphine – something that made no sense since it took me away from where I was ultimately heading, a 63 bus stop on Rue des Écoles.

"So, my darling, what *are* you up to?"

What had happened was simple enough. I had set off for a gallery where my friend Hugh Weiss was having a show; after that I planned to pick up some wine I'd had set aside at the Nicolas outlet at Sèvres-Babylone. As soon as I'd sat down on the bus I realized I'd forgotten my checkbook and got off at the next stop to go back for it; but I saw I was by then farther from home than from the gallery, so I decided I might as well go on, which meant taking the next bus. At the gallery I found out that Hugh's show had been rescheduled for the following week. I spent some time wandering around the the neighborhood before finally making up my mind to go back home.

What I said to Marie-Claude was, "You know how absent-minded writers are – I guess I'm no exception," adding with stagy casualness, "still, tell your friend that in his shoes I'd be careful (*je ferais attention*). One thing, Marie-Claude – did your father ever get my thank-you note for taking care of me at the hospital?"

"I see," said Marie-Claude.

Who was Marie-Claude's snoopy friend? He sounded like someone who was ready to take the bait. If he did, he'd become the star witness of my new life.

On Wednesday the week after, I attended Hugh Weiss's postponed opening. Marie-Claude was there, too. I spent time talking to Hugh and his circle until I saw Marie-Claude going by herself to the bar in the rear of the gallery. I quickly joined her and wasted no time asking her if her inquisitive friend happened to be with her. She pointed him out across the room. She didn't offer to introduce us, which was just as well. I wasn't interested in knowing him – I wanted to see him.

I saw him again the following morning when I went to buy my *Herald Tribune* at the local newspaper stand. He was sitting in Le Saint Germain, a café on the corner of Boulevard Raspail, drinking coffee and reading his own paper. I hoped this might be a daily ritual.

It was a daily ritual. The next three mornings I took a seat at the back of Le Saint Germain at nine o'clock. Marie-Claude's friend showed up regularly between 9:30 and 10 A.M. I was pleased that he showed no sign of recognizing me. I remember reading on my third morning that after resigning as ambassador to France, Pablo Neruda had declared that he would now devote himself entirely to "singing the glory of the Chilean people and the virtues of the country's workers."

The following Monday I started passing the Saint Germain *without* going in. I carried a briefcase and walked briskly west down Boulevard Saint-Germain. On the corner of Rue Saint-Simon I stopped in the recessed doorway of a bookstore and looked back. No sign of my mark, not the first morning or the next; on the third he was there. I led him by a devious route – Rues de Bellechasse, Varenne, Bourgogne, Las-Cases – to the church of Sainte Clothilde. I walked slowly and expectantly round the little park in front of the church. Then I hurried home a quite different way. I made sure I never lost my tail.

That afternoon I took the metro to Saint Augustin on the right bank. I got straight into a taxi that deposited me, back on the other side of town, near an Avis garage in the fifteenth arrondissement. I rented their cheapest model, a Peugeot 204. For half an hour I had fun practicing "evasive driving techniques" before heading for Sainte Clothilde. I pulled into the first space that opened up on the park side of Rue Marignan. Before leaving I cracked the rear window next to the sidewalk, left the same door unlocked, and pasted a two-inch strip of Scotch tape over its lower edge.

Next morning I led Marie-Claude's friend back to Sainte Clothilde, this time by way of Place du Palais-Bourbon. Again I walked slowly around the little park. Reaching Rue Marignan, I drew a plain envelope from the outer pocket of my briefcase and as I passed the rental car slipped it through the rear window. (I'd practiced the maneuver and didn't even break stride.) I went straight home once I'd looked back and made sure my man had reached the car. I knew I could count on him. Soon he'd be reading the typewritten page inside the envelope:

> In the wake of last week's disappointments, aggressive behavior produced results.
>
> After practicing savage and unnecessary provocation, Saint Sulpice escaped with a single penalty box. Port Royal demonstrated team cohesion and discipline.
>
> Port Royal showed an unfamiliar maturity: fierce but shrewd. Pascal and Racine led the way, followed closely by Fénelon (a revelation – old dog up to new tricks).
>
> Dependable Quesnel had to be replaced by Sévigné. Grignan and Corneille did excellent covering. La Rochefoucauld and La Fayette kept things moving forward and their slick diversions allowed Fénelon to score, finding his range on the third try: Bossuet will no longer be a problem.
>
> This performance gives Port Royal many reasons to be cheerful. Our strength in depth and collective resolve bodes well for next week's tricky visit to Sainte Chapelle.

That evening I went back to Saint Sulpice by taxi. My friend's friend was nowhere to be seen. The tape on the car door was broken; the envelope had been carefully resealed but was slightly torn at one corner. It was my forty-third birthday, and I had a good reason to celebrate. I'd shown that I could perform successfully in the game I'd chosen to play. This more than made up for the news that the dollar (i.e., my purchasing power) had just been devalued by ten percent.

Even if I liked playing spy, mid-winter in Paris is a forlorn season. Public places are depressingly empty after the holiday spending spree. The first six weeks of the year had been cold and clear, at least as clear as damp and polluted air allowed, but the weather turned warmer and rusty sunshine gave way to cloud and fog. The first cases were reported of what was then called *la grippe anglaise* and later Hong Kong flu. I felt I was catching not the flu but the gloom. I started worrying, and I did have something to worry about: I hadn't begun to solve the problem of cover. Not having cover might not have kept a lot of people from thinking I was CIA, but it made for an absurd situation. The trouble was, getting any kind of regular job meant applying for a work permit, and that was a long and very undependable procedure. Starting a business was a bureaucratic nightmare and would inevitably involve the *fisc* (the French IRS) with every detail of my life. I couldn't even ask a friend (for instance one of the gallery owners I knew) to give me part-time unofficial employment, because for a job to qualify as cover it had to be out in the open for all to see.

Meanwhile it had been snowing in the Vercors, a massif in the Alpine foreland where I'd bought a house fifteen years before. Three feet of snow had fallen in the villages, six feet on the upper slopes. I took a train to Grenoble, where a friend met me and drove me home; home being a hillside farmhouse outside Lans-en-Vercors, 3500 feet high, with fields in front of it and woods behind. By 10:30 next morning I was sliding down a sunny mountain above the nearby town of Villard-de-Lans.

In the Vercors you ski at relatively low altitudes – 2500 to 6000 feet – and this has one advantage: only the highest tows take you where there's nothing but snow and rock; most of the time you do runs dropping 2500 feet through forests of spruce and fir. The skiing that morning was exhilarating; and it seemed to stimulate thinking the way hiking always did: so that when I crossed the glistening expanse of Pré des Prés on my third run, I realized at last what my cover would be.

The problem was essentially one of appearances. Since I couldn't get a bona fide job, I'd invent an independent line of work that would validate itself; and it might as well be work that could be considered useful for intelligence business.

Two qualities are required of an intelligence officer in the field: placement and access, that is, knowing where information can be found and how to get it. What activity could supply those qualities? Something involving travel, especially travel to Iron Curtain countries. If I worked for CIA, I could run a real travel agency; short of that, couldn't I set myself up as a travel *advisor*? Thus a new and necessary entity was born on the last schuss of my trail: *Locus Solus – International Travel Counsel.*

The name was the clincher. *Locus Solus* had been a little magazine I'd started thirteen years before with three poet friends (it was originally the title of a work by one of our idols, Raymond Roussel). The magazine was officially published in Lans-en-Vercors or, rather, unofficially: then as now I wanted to avoid bureaucratic hassle, and I managed to persuade the quiet, friendly man who ran – and was still running – the local post office to let me use my personal address as the magazine's.

I went up on the ski lift to try another piste. I was pleased with the cover I'd chosen. Having the business in Lans would help protect it from nosey Parisian friends (it would incidentally justify my spending time in the mountains, something I loved doing). Working in the domain of travel would supply me with an obvious "paper mill," the name given in the trade to the succession of documents a good agent is expected to supply. My own paper mill would be made up of the traveler's basic tool: maps. When the time came, I'd make it clear that *my* maps were chock full of political and economic information – even geographical information, since it was no secret that the Soviet Union's official maps were falsified, especially those of Central Siberia. That way I could claim the appearance of "access."

I saw that I was already looking beyond my first aim of convincing the world I was a spy to virtually acting like one.

At the top of the Villard ski lift, there's a pleasant hostel called the Cote 2000, and I went in there for a lunch of cured mountain ham, beet-and-endive salad, and flinty white *vin de Savoie.* I skied under the bare sun until the snow started to soften. At home I went to work designing my commercial stationery and drafting the presentation I would use to launch my enterprise.

After a while I began wondering what close friends would think of my founding a travel business. Georges Perec, André du Bouchet, Henry and Judy Pillsbury, John and Chantal Hunt all knew I'd never been CIA. They'd tell me my scheme was as idiotic as the worries behind it. So to them I'd say I was simply helping out a deserving acquaintance; I'd only supplied a name and address for the business and agreed to hold an honorary position in it.

My "deserving acquaintance" might as well add to the mystery of the undertaking; so at the top of the masthead the Executive Director was given the unmistakably Polish name of Elzbieta

Sosnowska, followed by those of Sinclair Dillon, Treasurer (likewise invented) and Harry Mathews, Secretary. Correspondence was to be directed to the secretary's office in Lans-en-Vercors. In my presentation I asserted that this "town" (pop. 800) lay at the very center of western Europe, which might have been true for crows, wild boars, and helicopters. However, I emphasized that the scope of Locus Solus was worldwide: "Travel in our day is being channeled into standard itineraries. Our concern is for the exceptional traveler with unusual requirements, whether they take him to Bolivia, Hungary, or Outer Mongolia." I kept the rest short and vague.

In the morning I visited our postmaster. He hadn't forgotten my magazine. I explained that it had included a travel section, and that this had belatedly led to a confidential monthly letter sent out to subscribers – hence the addition of "international travel counsel" to the original title. He agreed to let me go on using my own address for business correspondence.

I drove down to Grenoble and bought the best answering machine available. I made sure it had a large storing capacity and a state-of-the-art mechanism for retrieving messages at a distance.

Paris came into view through the train window as a cluster of grimy lights dismally shrouded by rain. I'd had a few more days of blue-weather skiing before deciding it was time to get to work. During the five-hour ride, I caught up on news I'd missed. Israel was being slammed again, this time for shooting down a Libyan airliner over Sinai. Right-wing French groups were merging in something called the Front National. Marshal Pétain's coffin had been stolen from its tomb on Ile d'Yeu but recovered soon afterwards.

Early next morning I went to a little stationer's around the corner on Rue du Bac; I knew the owner did printing for local businesses. He gave me useful advice about fonts and layouts for my new stationery.

I had a chance to publicize Locus Solus that same day. I belonged to an organization called AARO, the Association of Americans Resident Overseas. (I'd joined it because its members had access to good medical coverage.) In the morning mail I found AARO's yearly form letter requesting recommendations for its Professional Directory. I entered my information about "Locus Solus – International Travel Counsel" and had the form back in the mail by noon. Not much was likely to come of it, I knew, but it couldn't hurt.

Marie-Claude's friend had reported what happened at Sainte Clothilde, and Marie-Claude had not kept the news to herself. People were starting to treat me differently. I wasn't being needled any more. My latest story was that I'd applied for a DAAD fellowship in West Berlin – the DAAD was a German government department that invited artists and writers to a place that was famous for intelligence and counterintelligence activity. A month before this would have had my listeners snickering; now they just nodded their heads.

I kept embellishing my new persona. I carried a piece of pink chalk in my pocket and I'd sometimes stop in out-of-the-way streets to scribble a cryptic sign on a wall. I spent forty francs at the used-goods market in Village Suisse on an aluminum suitcase pasted with labels not just from Gstaad and Amalfi but Bucarest and Leningrad. I left it next to the umbrella stand by my front door, where no one could miss noticing it.

I started seeing old French acquaintances again and enjoying it. This wasn't directly due to my becoming a semi-official spy – after all, no one could *approve* of my being CIA. What made the difference was the new confidence I'd acquired. I was playing my own private game, and that made me feel safe. I started seeing the world differently, especially the network of high-powered intellectuals that included so many of the people I knew.

I'd enjoyed reading Roland Barthes, Foucault, and early Derrida; if Lacan was tough going, I was at home with Freud and Marx. But when I discussed these authors with my French companions, I found out I hadn't understood them at all. On top of which came the implication that the important points, the points I'd missed, were ones I'd never grasp. I was made to feel like a conceptual bonehead.

I now was beginning to see that what my intellectual friends cared about was not anything I needed or wanted. They may have had the answers. I noticed, however, that their answers frequently came from commentators on the authors they revered rather than from the authors themselves – they were like students taking refuge in essays on Shakespeare instead of tackling *Hamlet* on their own. They reminded me of 4th-century Manicheans who hoped that if they ate a fig from the right tree they might eventually sigh forth some particles of the Godhead. My friends were looking for the figs of intellectual correctness. For me, what mattered was not the rightness of the ideas I'd collected but the process of thinking, something that often led to confusion – in my opinion, a very productive state of mind. So I went on listening to the talk about post-structuralism or Maoist theory, as interested as ever, but keeping my mouth shut, unless there was an urgent reason for me to open it.

One evening at La Coupole I joined a tableful of young writers and their companions, eight or nine in all, each as cute as can be. We gossiped. I confessed to my recent election to the Oulipo – Jean-Noël Vuarnet, who was then squiring the luscious Sylviane Agacinski, reminded me how outraged I'd been when he'd first told me about the group. A pretty woman, visibly pregnant, sat down with us. A less-pretty redhead facing me asked her, as soon as she had the chance, "What's it like, carrying death inside you for nine whole months?" Anyone with even a third-hand knowledge of Lacan knew what she meant; but the pregnant woman turned pale in dismay. I growled, "Just because *your* mother felt that way . . ." The others laughed, the pregnant woman smiled, the redhead scowled and kept quiet.

Someone once said that evil is only the corruption of knowledge. The redhead was more dumb than vicious. She'd found fashionable new ideas to be dumb with. I liked nuts, balls, birds, and whatever else life had to offer better than intellectual salvation. It was my world now, all mine.

Except for one thing: I was still in thrall to womankind. I thought I'd be miserable if I had to give up the embraces not of some women but of *all* women. I couldn't acknowledge that I'd lately been doing exactly that, with no apparent misery. My anxiety was an addiction, and it hooked me every time I went out. That evening I was sitting next to a willowy brunette with big wondering eyes – never mind the rest. I interested her; she'd probably been told I was a spook. The later it got, the closer we sat. I knew we'd soon be lying in each other's arms, and we would have been if I'd been willing to travel. She was taking the night train to Montpellier.

That was how it went in mid-winter 1973. No scores, and all my darlings out of town skiing, or staying warm in Martinique, or going steady.

My stationer called me on Monday, March 5 to tell me my order was ready. It was the day after the first round in France's municipal elections. As usual, the Communists got the most votes.

I was home typing my first letter on the new stationery when a man at AARO phoned. He'd read the description of Locus Solus I'd submitted for their directory. Would I consider helping a group of AARO members who had come to him for advice? They had a distressing problem in common: travel-stress dyslexia.

These men and women, perhaps a dozen in all, were well-educated and professionally successful Americans who'd settled in the Paris area. They depended on travel for work or pleasure or both. They'd all learned how to handle their congenital dyslexic condition; but in moments of stress – notably when they were setting off on a trip – their handicap resurfaced. It took the form of a common but peculiarly inconvenient dysfunction: they couldn't distinguish reading left to right from right to left. Deciphering travel schedules became impossible. Particularly critical breakdowns were apt to occur in train stations.

I was offered a decent fee. I agreed to give a talk on the subject under AARO's auspices. I had no inkling of what I would say, but I wasn't going to miss a chance of going public.

Two days later I attended the monthly meeting of the Oulipo, the second since I'd been elected to it. The Oulipo: in full, the Ouvroir de Littérature Potentielle or Workshop for Potential Literature, a group of writers, scholars, and mathematicians founded by Raymond Queneau and François Le Lionnais in 1960. Its purpose was to explore the *potentialities* mathematics might contribute to literature. I'd been introduced to the group by Georges Perec, who had published a notorious Oulipian work – a full-length novel in which the letter e never appeared.

Among those who had gathered at François Le Lionnais's that morning was an Oulipian called Luc Étienne. He was an expert in verbal acrobatics – palindromes, lipograms, salacious spoonerisms. He presented us with a bilingual palindrome. It was modest enough but a first for him and for the Oulipo: when reversed, *"T'es sûr, Ned dort nu ?"* became "untrodden russet." I wasn't much impressed or even interested until it occurred to me that numerical palindromes might solve travel-stress dyslexia. Numbers were not merely bi- but multilingual; and any number could be read backwards. Once I was home it didn't take me long to formulate the principles of what I was going to tell the AARO audience.

Of course principles wouldn't be enough. They had to be turned into practical possibilities. I spent a day in travel agencies, including several specializing in countries behind the Iron Curtain. Then over the weekend I scoured every page in the Thomas Cook *Overseas Railway and Road Services Guide* for information. By the time I finished I'd compiled more material than I needed.

I GAVE MY TALK AT 6 P.M. THAT TUESDAY. AARO HAD RENTED a small conference room on the second floor of the Travellers Club, on the Champs-Élysées. My sponsor introduced me briefly. I stood behind a collapsible aluminum reading stand in front of thirty-odd people. Almost all of them were conservatively dressed American men. It was an older crowd, with one noticeably pretty young woman in jeans. It felt like a friendly audience.

Good evening to one and all. I expressed my sympathy for anyone who had come here for help. Departure anxiety was familiar to most of us, certainly to me – I always seemed to be catching planes and trains with either two hours or ten seconds to spare. I could easily understand how anyone with a dyslexic past might be panicked into a relapse when they were confronted with an array of departure times that made such hopelessly different sense depending on their being read forwards or backwards. Was I right, I asked, in imagining that the problem arose more often in train and bus stations, where schedules were printed or posted, than in airports, where flights were generally announced in English as well as the local language?

Several members of the audience nodded. In that case, I went on, here were two rules that would allow them in future to travel free of all anxiety.

Rule one: *they should only take trains and buses whose departure times read the same right to left as they did left to right.* This was perfectly doable thanks to the 24-hour clock used almost universally outside America, where 13:00 means 1 P.M., 14:00 2 P.M. and so forth. On any day they'd have sixteen possibilites:

01:10
02:20
03:30
04:40
05:50
10:01
11:11
12:21
13:31
14:41
15:51
20:02
21:12
22:22
23:32
00:00

These departure times covered the entire day, with only two gaps in mid morning and late afternoon. I knew from experience that trains were as apt to leave at odd-seeming times like 10:01 as on the hour or half-hour. Admittedly buses were more of a problem: frequently midnight (00:00) was the only acceptable time available.

(I felt I had to mention, but *not* recommend, two other series of departure times. First, 03:33, 04:44, and 05:55. Since we all know that there are only twenty-four hours in the day, these numbers when turned around obviously had to be repunctuated to be practical, e.g., 33:30 to 3:33(0). Second, 07:07, 08:08, and 09:09, where both the minute and the hour columns had to be similarly reinterpreted, e.g., 70:70 to 7:07(0). But I warned that performing these manipulations under stress was dangerous. The only infallible times were the sixteen primary ones.)

Rule two: *for every departure, a return must be assured that strictly obeys rule one.* Otherwise difficulties and even disasters were inevitable. I was dedicating my present talk to Auguste Blaise, a former dyslexic and client, who one day in October, 1968, against my urgent advice, had taken the 04:40 Island Express from Jolarpettai Junction to Bangalore and never been heard of again.

So much for basics. How did they work out in practice? I didn't have to fake my satisfaction (it *had* been hard work) when I outlined dozens of trips that could be taken in Latin America, Asia, even Africa. (One of them, I admitted – two days' risky travel in Zaïre between Dilolo and Kolwesi – was included simply to illustrate my point.) Surprisingly, I added, two very attractive countries had to be excluded from their travel plans: there wasn't a safe trip available in India, in spite of its huge rail network, or in Mexico, even though it was crisscrossed with bus routes. For instance, it was easy to reach Mexico City by midnight bus from almost any part of the country; but there was no way of getting out of it.

These examples, I went on, involved simple connections between two or three places; extended itineraries offered much more rewarding possibilities. I demonstrated what I meant by describing in detail how one could travel around Brazil by bus, from Rio to Belo Horizonte to São Paolo and back to Rio, with numerous safe excursions on the way. Departure times were invaribly 00:00 – who could ask for more?

At this point I noticed that several people in the audience were taking notes and only two were asleep. I was ready with my crown jewel.

"I would like to conclude by presenting my favorite itinerary of all. It doesn't take you through any of the regions I've mentioned thus far. No, it takes you to the heart of the most mysterious nation on the planet: a round trip from Moscow to Krasnoyarsk, with stops at Sverdlovsk, Omsk, and Novosibirsk. If so desired, it can be extended as far as Irkutsk."

I briefly described the conditions of Soviet train travel. I added that for the first leg of the journey, from Moscow to Sverdlovsk, there was an alternate, less direct route which I didn't recommend but that I thought I should at least indicate: "Departure from Moscow at 05:55 – you notice that this time belongs to the low-security category – on the Kuzbass Express, which has 1st and 2nd classes, a dining car, and European sleepers in 1st class. Arrival in Kirov in the afternoon two days later. Departure from Kirov at 22:22, 2nd class, fast. Arrival in Perm II next day. Departure from Perm II at 14:41, 2nd class, fast, bringing you to Sverdlovsk early the following morning."

(I'd included this alternative because I was nourishing an unlikely hope that people in touch with the intelligence community might be present: to them it would sound preposterous. No foreigner would ever be allowed near Perm II – it was a major nuclear center whose existence was barely acknowledged.)

"Here is the normal, recommended way of making the trip. You leave Moscow at 23:32, on a train that unfortunately is only 2nd or 'hard' class – but it is at least 'fast hard-class.' You reach Sverdlovsk three days later at 05:50 (isn't that a delightful coincidence?). You can spend your time there visiting the traditional gemstone-cutters or, if you're historically minded, inspect the site where the imperial family was massacred on the night of July 16, 1918.

"You leave Sverdlovsk at 03:30 on – and I'm sure you will be pleased to hear this – the Kafaikalye, an express train with dining car and sleepers. That same afternoon you will be in Omsk. The city sits at the confluence of the Ob and Irtych rivers – the latter humorously referred to by the Tsarist Admiral Kolchak as the 'kingdom of Irtych' when during the civil war he chucked a number of socialist moderates into its waters. Some travelers recommend a visit to the veterinary institute. By the way, in spite of occasional violent snowfalls and sandstorms, the climate is considered clement.

"Another comfortable train takes you from Omsk at 10:01 to Novosibirsk the next morning. A real metropolis, Novosibirsk – opera, ballet, botanical gardens, you name it – and, for those so inclined, in nearby Akademgorok there are several research institutes and a major branch of the Academy of Sciences.

"On from Novosibirsk at 22:22 with, I'm sorry to say, a 2nd-class only train, getting to Krasnoyarsk two days later in the early hours. This is also a major city, with another branch of the Academy of Sciences. But its main attraction is the dam, one of the largest in the world (height 328 feet). It is, you should be warned, a *chilly* place; in fact the Yenisei stays frozen on the average for 160 days of the year.

"Krasnoyask is where you normally head back to Moscow, leaving at 14:41 (2nd class only) and getting there in one go five days later. But as I said before it is also possible to proceed on to Irkutsk with its lovely riversides and old wooden houses, not to mention its mica-processing factories – actually from Irkutsk you can if you feel like it keep going all the way to Beijing: it takes two days on a very comfortable train. But once you're in Beijing, there's no getting back to Moscow.

"Finally, I should point out one apparent disadvantage of this schedule, and let me emphasize the word 'apparent.' The timetables I've been quoting apply only to the period between November 1 and March 31. What you may not know and what you must remember is that winter in Siberia may be bad, but it's not nearly as bad as summer, when the temperature is in the hundreds, there's no air conditioning, and mosquitoes eat you alive if you as much as set foot out of doors.

"In any case, I'm sure the attractions of this exceptional journey are enough to outweigh its drawbacks in the eyes of travelers as curious and knowledgeable as yourselves, and that most of you will agree that this trip is definitely worth taking.

"Thank you for your attention. If you need more information, I can be reached locally at 222-8222. Questions?"

The sleepers woke up and joined in the polite applause. There probably would have been questions but by the time the clapping ended I'd been buttonholed by a stumpy man in his forties. He was wearing a black suit and white nylon shirt. He'd been staring at me through his metal-rimmed spectacles during all the last part of my talk. People were leaving; the young woman in jeans flashed me a smile on her way out.

The man said, "Very nervous plan."

"It makes you nervous?"

"Need much nerves. You know Plishkin?"

Another man joined us. He was younger and a lot pleasanter looking, in his gray Harris-tweed blazer, brown serge slacks, and black buckle shoes. "Excuse me, I don't want to interrupt, but I wanted to give you my card. I'm not a problem traveler, just a fan of your work." The card read Patrick Burton-Cheyne. He didn't stay.

"You speak with Tourist Department? You say many trains have no Intourist OK."

"May I ask your name, sir?"

"Eugenius Schmidt."

"The Soviet project worries you, Mr. Schmidt?"

"Exact. Project will provoke – you know this. You think traveling people go to places? You think to go too?"

"The concept appeals to me."

"Concept! You are maybe attract by thrill of acting against law? You know Plishkin?"

"Plishkin – "

"Perm II! And Sverdlovsk – with nearby Area 1 of Nizhaya Tura Atomic Energy Complex. In northeast outskirt of Novosibirsk other atomic complex, next line of Trans-Siberian. Always I think all is matter for doubt. But in plan appears very much – " He searched for a word. "When two factors join in single phenomenon – "

"Coincidence?"

"Coincidence, thank you. You know Plishkin back at work?"

An overcoat over one arm, the man from AARO stopped to thank me and hand me my check. The room had emptied. I looked at my watch and said I had a pressing appointment. This was so: Régine was opening at the Bobino later that evening. Friends had recently introduced me to her at her famous nightclub. I'd told her I'd never heard her sing, and she'd reserved a seat for me tonight.

"Thank you, H. Mathews. *A bientôt*," said E. Schmidt, shaking my hand. Where in the world did he think we'd meet again?

I MANAGED TO GET TO THE BOBINO IN TIME FOR A GIN-AND-TONIC at the theater bar. I was then seated anonymously among the chic and famous. The show wasn't bad – sharp production, stylish charm from Régine, a lot of laughs from Claude Véga, who went on first. I kept thinking: why would anyone want to call himself Eugenius Schmidt?

I was hungry when I left the theater. I walked down the street to Les Iles Marquises and ate a dozen oysters, grilled golden bream (*daurade*), a portion of Munster, and a half followed by a full bottle of Riesling.

I'd eaten at the back of the restaurant. On my way out I passed a big table near the front where Régine was sitting. Next to her was Barbara, another singer whose name was enough to bring tears to my eyes; and then a younger woman, a long-haired brunette with full lips and breasts. I stopped when I saw her. I stared at her, then at the others, and all three stared back at me. I felt myself blushing hard. I had to say something, anything –*"Bravo! Mille bravos! Ah oui, madame, bravo! Et merci, je ne sais comment vous dire, encore merci!"* Régine thanked me for coming; Barbara yawned; the brunette looked at me as if I were Mortimer Snerd.

For weeks I thought of that look, and her. But I was too embarrassed by what had happened to phone Régine to ask who she was.

Winter was ending blustery and wet. I decided to spend part of my AARO fee (500 francs) on good Bordeaux; I found out it cost four times as much as two years before. Inflation was taking over, the dollar had been devalued twice in a few months, the Dow-Jones was at 963 and still sinking. It would be nice if Locus Solus could keep bringing in some money. For twenty years I'd managed well on my modest capital, but it was shrinking fast.

After my AARO talk I started going to movies with friends – I remember seeing *Last Tango in Paris* and *Flesh.* One evening I went alone to Salle Gaveau for a Schumann recital by Gérard Souzay. (I'd heard him sing the *Dichterliebe* in Nice exactly twenty years earlier.) In the lobby I ran into Patrick Burton-Cheyne, the man who'd left his card with me at the Travellers Club.

We had a drink together. Eight years ago he'd been a graduate student at Duke and written a controversial doctorate on "Traded Craft in the Work of Eliot and Ashbery," and it was through Ashbery that he'd come to read my novels. He wished someone would write about my own "œuvre."

"Two books and a mimeographed sheaf of poems an œuvre do not make."

"Why leave out *The Sinking*? Because it appeared in a magazine? If I had time these days I'd do it myself."

He worked for Zapata Petroleum. I asked, wasn't that a kind of oxymoron? "It's a big company all right. It was started by the Liedtke brothers and George Bush – you know, Nixon's last ambassador to the UN? He's just replaced Dole as GOP chairman.

By the way, do you like opera?" He had an extra ticket for a visiting East German production of *Fidelio* at the end of the month. I wasn't going to turn that down.

As we were saying goodbye, Patrick asked me, "That weird guy who came up to talk to you the other night – what was he after?"

"I think he was worried about going to Perm II."

"You can't blame him. Take care."

I felt at loose ends in the daytime. Going places by roundabout ways and writing on blank walls didn't amount to an occupation, and I kept wishing that Locus Solus would bring me another windfall like the AARO talk.

I began writing again. Nothing ambitious, a few experiments with methods I'd learned from the Oulipo. That and going to the movies and dining with friends weren't enough, however, to erase the image of the young woman I'd glimpsed at Les Iles Marquises.

Late one morning I heard an unfamiliar woman's voice on the phone. The voice was low and clear and said, "Monsieur Mathews? Marie-Claude Quintelpreaux. We once met – I think you don't remember. I also went to your lecture, that's what I'm calling about."

"You were wearing jeans?"

"Yes. I was there because of my brother."

"He has travel problems?"

"Not dyslexia. He's a recluse. A very obstinate one. It's hard even getting him to go out. I think your funny scheme might appeal to him. If I can set up a meeting at my place, would you be willing to come? Naturally I'll take care of your fee."

I noted her address and phone number. We agreed on a day and time.

I hung up. The phone rang again: "Hello, it's Marie-Claude."

"Oh – there's a problem?"

"Harry, does there have to be a problem?" Two voices so alike – but this could not be Marie-Claude Quintelpreaux. Marie-Claude Podopoulos was calling to say that her *ami* was out of town. What about dinner tonight?

If I'd had a date I would have broken it. My affair with Marie-Claude had been kept alive by impromptu meetings like this. A meal followed by deliberate, intense love-making that could last a day or a night and beyond. Right now that was an alluring prospect.

We had a pleasant dinner at Chez Joséphine on Rue du Cherche-Midi. But I went home alone. Marie-Claude had wanted to tell me that her friend was the man of her life: she was marrying him. She didn't want me to hear the news from anyone else. For once I had the sense not to spoil things by pushing too hard.

I realized how lonely I'd been feeling. It was not only sex. I craved the warmth that only intimacy with a woman could bring. Spring was coming on, and that made me more melancholy than ever.

Later that week Georges Perec took an evening off from filming *Un Homme qui dort*. It did me good to see him. He'd always laughed at the way I ran after women, and now he cheered me up by making fun of my "loneliness." He gave me some practical help, too. When I told him about the brunette at Les Iles Marquises, he suggested I go back to the restaurant: "They'll know who she is." After dinner we went to his place to smoke pot and listen to music. Only a few takes of Coleman Hawkins this time: my friend was a weary man.

Early the following evening I returned to Les Iles Marquises. I felt lucky to find the same headwaiter on duty. He vaguely remembered me (one customer, two bottles of wine . . .); he certainly remembered Régine's party. I explained that I had been fascinated by the young woman sitting next to Barbara and was curious to learn who she was. I knew Régine only slightly and hesitated to approach her on the subject. Perhaps he could help me out.

"I remember the young lady well," the headwaiter answered with an understanding smile. "A striking girl. I've no idea who she is. The patron may know, He was here that evening, and he's a friend of Barbara's. He's away for a couple of weeks on vacation – he loves spring skiing – but I can ask him when he comes back. Where can you be reached?"

I wrote down my phone number and handed it to him together with a hundred-franc bill. He accepted it with aplomb.

I had my appointment with Marie-Claude Quintelpreaux the following afternoon. It was a warm, sunny Saturday; I decided to walk to her place, just past Luxembourg Gardens on Rue Abbé de l'Épée.

On the way I thought about the job she was giving me. I couldn't really believe that palindromic departure times would persuade her reclusive brother to take a train to Moscow. Better start with something simpler, like walking around Paris. Such obsessive reclusiveness suggested a hangover from childhood; but the persistence of a childish terror didn't exclude the memory of childish enthusiams. Perhaps I could call on them as a way of getting the reluctant brother out of doors. What about the saga of the three musketeers? Every boy in France had thrilled to their story. Why not propose exploring places associated with them, the places for instance where the four heroes had lived? That would cover a lot of territory, from the musketeer barracks on Rue de Montreuil to Athos's lodgings on Rue Férou, barely a hundred yards from the point I'd now reached, where a riot policeman was barring the way into Luxembourg Gardens.

The park was closed "to all youths between the ages of 15 and 40." My driver's license convinced him I wasn't even a forty-year-old youth. I'd forgotten about the series of student protests against the Loi Debré, which threatened to eliminate exemptions from military service. They were climaxing today in a march down Boulevard St.-Michel (200,000 strong, I later read). That's what I somehow had to get past on the far side of the park.

It could have been worse. I arrived only ten minutes late, but I wished I hadn't been sweating so visibly when I rang the bell.

Marie-Claude Quintelpreaux lived on the ground floor of a roomy 19th-century building. The front rooms of her apartment were dark, the ones in back flooded with light from the big walled lawn beyond. She took me into the smaller and darker of two living rooms. It smelled of sandalwood incense. There was something in one corner that looked like a little shrine, with lighted candles flickering on it. The floor was covered with soft Tibetan rugs. We sat on leather poufs facing one another.

Marie-Claude quickly confessed to a ruse: there was no brother. She had met me last December at Mark Rudkin's on Rue Monsieur. "You still don't remember!" She had come late, which meant I'd been drinking all evening and might have forgotten many things; but her luminous red-blond hair and shapely half-smiling mouth, her gentian-blue eyes? I told her: not possible.

She said, *"Vous me plaisez beaucoup."* Her formal *vous* carried great erotic authority. I went on sweating. She bent forward and rested her fingernails below my ears, then kissed me at sufficient length. I settled down. Slow caresses followed. They could only lead to one sure thing.

"Stop," Marie-Claude gently but firmly pulled away, "stop, stop, stop. My darling, it is too marvelous. It is very rare. We must bring it to perfection, we must make it last—"

"Of course, we'll take all the time you want—"

"Yes, a long time. Not just minutes, not even hours: days. Until the unquestionable moment . . ."

I remembered the incense, the shrine – was I being seduced to partake of the Wisdom of the East? I thought: she's going to want to sublimate everything. Transcendance, transformation, yes, yes, but not now. Tantric yoga now was *unfair.*

I was starting to say so when Marie-Claude stood up and gave her shoulders a little shake; her blue caftan gathered at her feet; she stood there in what the French called the simplest of apparels. I didn't say anything. What I saw was worth waiting for as long as she liked.

She told me to get undressed. She had us kneel face to face: "Closer, not touching but almost. Your lips very close to mine, so, we tilt our heads first to the right so our mouths make an x, then breathe out and say om on one long note. No, just let it float out. Then the head goes to the opposite side . . ." The tip of my erection settled in her navel; this was apparently acceptable. I thought, "There's no place like om." I lost track of time. Our drone soon was emanating not from us but from the space around us. I saw myself inside her first through one slanting eye then the other. My spine started unwinding upwards through my skull. Maybe she was onto something.

So I survived, with my desire more than intact. "You will come back soon." I understood that it was she who would tell me when.

Three days later I met Patrick at the Théâtre des Champs-Élysées to hear *Fidelio*. I invited him afterwards to supper at the Bar des Théâtres on the other side of Avenue Montaigne – it was small and pleasant, a nice place to get to know somebody. We found we had lots to agree about, starting with Theo Adam's sterling Pizarro; then good wine (we were drinking a '66 Côte de Beaune) and good food; and living in France. As it turned out, we loved almost every kind of music, and musical theater particularly. It was comforting to know that he'd enjoyed reading my work.

We closed the place at one A.M. Over our last drink Patrick said he was going to Milan on business in two weeks; and he had tickets to La Scala. Why didn't I come along?

I'd never been there; I agreed at once. "But let me take care of the hotel." Patrick recommended the Hotel della Scala, on the same square as the opera. I told myself: Locus Solus will now strut its stuff.

Next morning I reserved two rooms for us at the hotel, then phoned the Italian Tourist Bureau for the name of the hotel's manager: Dottore Gabriele Mannoni. I wrote him a letter asking him to extend every possible consideration to the secretary of Locus Solus and his traveling companion during their forthcoming visit. The travel counsel service would of course continue to direct its clients to the hotel, whose high standards of comfort and service were well established. The letter was typed on Locus Solus stationery and signed Elzbieta Sosnowska.

Dott. Mannoni replied by letter quickly and courteously. He promised Madame Sosnowska to do all he could to make her friends welcome.

I was glad Locus Solus was again producing practical results. Having my game actively working brought me an advantage I hadn't been aware of before: it made me less vulnerable to public events. Writing had only rarely done that for me. In fact it had been writing that had first painfully exposed me to world affairs. I had started my first novel in September, 1956 – a doomed undertaking, stuck as I was in the belief that I had to conform to the conventional fiction I was familiar with. Struggling with this task, more and more frustrated with each passing day, to fill up the time I started reading newspapers compulsively – the *Herald Tribune*, *Le Monde*, *France-Soir*, and weeklies such as *L'Express* and *France-Observateur*, and anything else I could buy at a newsstand. I soon found myself dramatically overinformed about the succession of international crises that followed: rebellion in Poland, the Hungarian uprising, the attack on Nasserite Egypt by England and France to keep control of the Suez Canal. By reading so much about these events, not seeing that being overinformed generates only mental chaos, I became emotionally implicated in them – implicated and of course powerless to do anything about them. (One day in October Jean Tinguely and I went to the Red Cross headquarters in Paris to volunteer our services in Budapest. It was Saturday; their offices were closed.)

Feeling responsible for what western countries were doing elsewhere in the world survived this crazy initiation. I signed protests against France's policy of repression in Algeria and offered my apartment as a refuge for FLN fugitives; on trips back to the United States I devoted long cold hours marching against our war in Vietnam; but my bitterness and frustration were never allayed. More recently, instead of being simply angry at our bombing North Vietnam or invading Cambodia, I found myself cringing in personal shame. Now, playing my ridiculous spy game, my feelings changed. I didn't lose interest in events, in fact I followed them as closely as ever; but I no longer thought myself compromised by them.

There was still plenty to be interested in. The local student protests were turning violent – the protesters were being attacked by the Front National and Ordre Nouveau. In America the presidency we'd all once trusted went on sliding into disgrace. I thought it was emblematic of our decadence that in the week of Nixon's second inauguration the American League introduced the degrading position of designated hitter into baseball. I cared about such matters, but more the way I cared about catastrophes in the Peleponnesian Wars when I was reading Thucydides.

Sometimes political decisions were made that affected me personally. The Shah nationalized Iranian oil and raised its price sky-high, which was bound to make my money worth a lot less. Even here having my own game to play took the drama out of the prospect. I couldn't blame the Iranians for wanting their oil back; and I told myself that whatever happened, I'd be able to fend for myself – I'd learn how to write in ways that brought in a good income, or I'd find a paying job, if not here, then in the United States.

And sometimes the news was good. Every last GI was out of Vietnam; and if you believed the reviews, Paris was set to produce decent opera again.

I didn't mention my Milan trip to my friends, not even Georges. I only said I'd be away on business for a few days. Georges asked, "What's her name?"

Marie-Claude Quintelpreaux phoned twice before I left, but it wasn't to ask me back. I pleaded, "Why not?" "Everything in good time. I wanted to talk to you. Remember, when we meet, we won't be doing much talking."

I said I had nothing against talking to her. So we chatted. She asked me what I was doing, if I had any plans. I replied that aside from leaving town for a couple of days, I was busy attending to business.

"Where are you spending your 'couple of days'?" Italy, I told her. "Venice, I suppose. Or Tuscany? My absolute favorite."

"Milan, actually." I had no reason to hide the fact from her.

"Milan! I was supposed to be going there myself. But there's no way I can manage it."

I couldn't let my flash of hope disappear without protest. "Why not? We could go together. We'd be able to talk our hearts out," I added.

"I can't. I just can't." She paused. "Could you do me a favor?" Anything, I said. She'd been entrusted with a letter to be delivered personally to someone in Milan. "Could you deliver it for me?" Of course. "OK. It's for a man called – I can't remember his actual name, it'll be on the envelope, but he's generally known as Chisly Will. He hangs out in one of the cafés in the Galleria – the big arcade in the center of town. I'll write down the name of the café for you. Tell him the letter's from – " She pronounced a name I wasn't sure I'd caught.

"Sando?"

"That's close enough. I don't know the guy, he's the friend of a friend. I was advised to give him the letter and not stick around."

"I get the picture. When can I pick up this mysterious missive?"

“You stay right where you are! I’ll have a messenger bring it over tomorrow morning. Do I have your address?” I gave it to her. “A big thank you. I’ll call you as soon as you’re back.”

“Promise?”

She promised.

THE AIR-TRAFFIC CONTROLLERS HAD BEEN ON STRIKE FOR WEEKS, but some airlines had begun flying out of Orly. Patrick and I caught a late Alitalia flight to Linate.

Milan made Paris and its demos look like a kindergarten outing. Right-wing gangs (many of them bussed in from other regions) had taken over streets and squares and even one major highway into the city. All through the day – it was Tuesday, April 11 – there had been clashes between the police and left- and right-wing factions. Traffic was still a mess when we arrived. We didn't get to our hotel before ten.

Dottore Mannoni had waited for us. He showed us our accommodations himself – the best in the place, at the minimum rate. Patrick murmured, "Bravo, Locus Solus!" While we were unpacking, a bowl of fresh fruit and a bottle of iced champagne were brought to each of our rooms.

Patrick was off on business early next morning. The political uproar went on all day and only stopped after a right-winger's bomb killed one of the riot police (the *celere*) on Via Belotti. Moving around the city center wasn't too bad. I got to see Piero's "Virgin under the egg" again.

I met Patrick at the hotel late in the afternoon. There was more fruit and champagne, which we sampled before going across the square for our evening at La Scala. Not a great program – *Suor Angelica* and Dukas's *La Péri* – but at last I'd seen the inside of the legendary theater. The Puccini was wonderful; we decided to skip the ballet.

I'd already told Patrick how much I looked forward to eating at Savini's, a restaurant in the Galleria where my mother went on her first nights in Milan. She always ordered the same meal: *prosciutto di San Daniele*, *risotto alla milanese*, *cotoletta alla milanese* – as Patrick observed, she had a robust appetite. We soon walked into the bright lights of the great arcade.

I had Marie-Claude's letter in my pocket, and I was happy to have brought it with me when Patrick unexpectedly ran into a friend whose name I understood as Taglia. The two men greeted one another warmly. After being introduced, I asked Signor Taglia if he was a Milanese, which he said he was; and then if, by any chance, he knew of an habitué of the Galleria familiarly referred to as Chisly Will.

He interrupted: "My God, everyone knows Chisly Will." He looked in astonishment at Patrick, who shook his head and said, "Harry's OK." "You don't want to meet him, do you?" I explained that I had a letter to him from a friend. "Very well. You see that place right behind me? The Caffè Grande Italia, that's his headquarters. He's sitting there now, first table on the right as you go in. There are four other men with him – he's the baldish guy in the pale-gray suit. Please, watch your step! He's an eel."

Patrick said, "I'll wait for you at Savini's."

At the Grande Italia the five men looked up suspiciously when I approached. I bowed and handed over the letter: "From Sando." "Sando? Yes, yes, of course." Chisly Will stood up and shook hands. He gave me a fluorescent, ear-to-ear grin, not letting go of my hand: "You must join us!" I excused myself.

Patrick was sitting at a side table with two glasses of Prosecco. "Everything go all right? My friend tells me Chisly Will is a notorious grifter. That's all he knows."

In the course of the meal Patrick told me a little about himself. He'd gone straight from his literary studies into business. Working as a scholar had developed his talent for interpreting factual information, a valuable commodity in the oil industry, it turned out. Esso had hired him on a short contract to do background research on oil markets, and that's what he was doing now full-time for Zapata. He swore that his years exploring the subtleties of modernist poetry were what made him good at his job. He'd spotted the usefulness of applying the philosophy of Peirce and Husserl to the writing of Mallarmé and Stevens; now he investigated the incidence of alcoholism among the wives of Siberian workers and the funding of subversive movements in Pakistan when he prepared his forecasts of oil prices. He'd come to Milan because of Iran's nationalization of its oil; specifically, he was hoping to verify rumors about the Shah's ill health. He'd planned to contact a cousin of the Shah's personal physician who was studying law here. That hadn't happened, but he'd obtained useful information through another channel. The trip had been anything but a waste of time.

Several bombs exploded in the city that night and next morning. One of them killed Christa Knemius, a fugitive member of the Baader-Meinhof Gang, the group of left-wing terrorists responsible for a series of killings in Germany in 1972; she had been in hiding here for some time. We heard that a general strike had been called and thought we might well end up stuck in Milan; but the strike only lasted an hour. Our train, the Cisalpino, left on schedule at 3:30 P.M.

We had fine weather traveling up the western shore of Lago Maggiore to Domodossola and the tunnel under the Alps, and through Switzerland after that. A dining-car was attached to the train at Lausanne.

It was still light when we sat down at the table Patrick had been careful to reserve. We didn't go back to our seats until reached

Paris. Earlier Patrick had finished a draft of his report; we had plenty of time to talk.

Over dessert Patrick asked, "Did you have a personal reason for giving that talk in Paris? You say you're a travel counselor, but I can't imagine counseling people to spend days and nights crossing Siberia in winter on wooden seats. It doesn't figure."

I was abruptly filled with a desire to tell him the truth. Could I trust him? He had been unfailingly kind and open with me. When he was writing up his notes after leaving Milan, he'd even offered to share what he'd learned there – what the Shah's unannounced motives were in nationalizing his country's oil and why he was doomed to fail. I had demurred; but I was touched by his confidence in me: this was certainly confidential information. I didn't have doubts about wanting Patrick as a friend, especially since he'd be one with no connection to my circle of acquaintances; if I confided in him and he kept reasonably quiet there'd be no risk of having my spy persona jeopardized. His question made me realize how much I needed to tell someone about all I'd been doing. It had been exciting enough, but it was frustrating keeping the excitement to myself. Wasn't Patrick someone who could sympathize with the game I was playing and even appreciate it?

I told him the whole story: my unwished-for CIA rep, my deciding to make it work for me, my little tricks in Paris, and thinking up Locus Solus, which led to the AARO talk. "I thought the word might get out that I was taking a bunch of Americans on a tour of Soviet nuclear installations. Listen, does the name Plishkin mean anything to you?"

Patrick was laughing. He said that my passing for a CI agent was outrageous. "What you've managed to do is incredible. You have no access to anything!" As for Plishkin: "Siberia's one of my stamping grounds (not that I've ever been there). He's a big nuclear scientist. He got into trouble because he's scientist first and foremost and wants his research published. They can't really do without him, though, so for the time being he's being kept under house arrest somewhere in Khadistan. You hear something about him?"

"Eugenius Schmidt mentioned him three times."

"You know, Harry, I can actually help you out. What I do for a living is intelligence work pure and simple. I happen to be doing it for a commercial enterprise, not the government. But there are jobs where commercial enterprises are after the same stuff – you know CIA has to routinely prepare economic forecasts. We all end up using the same sources, and lots of times we go after them in the same ways. So if ever you need advice about how to act like a spy, about what you should be seen doing, I'm your man."

That suited me fine. We drank a toast – a third Armagnac – to our partnership.

I asked Patrick if there was anything particularly useful he could pass on to me "about the CIA." "The first thing to remember is that nobody connected with the Agency calls it *the* CIA. It's plain CIA."

He didn't tell me much about CIA's *modus operandi* that I hadn't heard already, but I did learn about the generally accepted laws of intelligence organizations. The basic rule is that if something can go wrong, it will. Applied to information from the field as it was read in supervisory offices, this means: "When something can be misinterpreted, it will be." Kent's law is more specific: "Any coup d'état I've heard about isn't going to happen." (Qaddafi's had come as a complete surprise.) The law of Excessive Approval means that when a review board responds to a report with unqualified enthusiasm it's headed for the shredder. Platt's law decrees that the final quantity of information in a report depends on whether the number of boards reviewing it is odd or even. "If the staff writes it long, the board wants it short, or vice versa; the next board wants the opposite of whatever the previous board asked for; and so it goes, from the first review board to the last."

"Does anything ever work?"

"If it does, they don't talk about it."

He made his final remarks as the train pulled into Gare de Lyon. "I think you should know what CIA wants its operatives to look like: absolutely unremarkable, middle-aged or older, average height, weak eyes blinking through glasses – the suburban commuter look. They would never have hired you."

"You neither." He was a tall, sharp-eyed redhead.

"You should organize commo for future occasions – even if you'll be the only one using it."

"What's that?"

"It's a word any CIA man would know. Places to meet on business. Museums, department stores."

I told him I was glad we didn't have to meet in places like that.

I SPENT THE WEEKEND PREPARING FOR THE OULIPO'S APRIL meeting on Tuesday. I wanted to present the experimental pieces I'd written, several of which had been accepted by a London poetry magazine. They were as Oulipian as can be; but they were in English. Nothing *wrong* with that, but I knew the Oulipo was much more responsive to work in French. So I toiled for three days concocting French replicas of my poems. This was hard but rewarding. Complying with my own rules allowed me to write the language with an assurance I'd never known before.

The Oulipo was pleased – I could tell this by Georges Perec's good humor. He always worried about blunders I was liable to make when I wrote in French, and I'd clearly done better than avoid disaster.

Back home, I was making coffee when Marie-Claude Quintelpreaux called and asked me to come over. That same afternoon. I took the fastest bath of my life, scrambled into low-key finery (gray cashmere pullover, snug black velvet bellbottoms), and ran down a taxi outside.

She took me into the same room. One long kiss – the only time we touched. We spent the next hour passing hands and mouths over every part of our naked bodies, slow and close. I wanted to sob like a little boy, then laugh, it was so silly; then I became fascinated. After all, we could mimic *anything*; we could improvise as perversely as we liked. There were times – for instance, feeling her breath on my scrotum – when I thought my desire would expand into something like its own consummation. At the end I was elated. Confused, too, beyond words; at least any words I knew.

I'D RECENTLY STARTED RETRIEVING MESSAGES FROM MY ANSWERING machine in Lans, all from the same few businessmen. Their names were new to me. When I called them, they were vague about how they'd heard of Locus Solus. One of them did know Patrick.

I met them at their offices or, if they were from out of town, their hotel rooms, sometimes in a bar. They were all Americans and emphasized the fact – "We certainly ought to be able to work together." To find out what they were after – I knew it wasn't travel advice – I always spoke evasively until they began showing their hand. What all of them were after was information. They assumed I was an "expert" or an "authority." What they in fact assumed was that I was CIA. Locus Solus was convincing cover after all.

Of course I had no information. So I stalled. I developed into a good staller by stumbling onto an effective technique. Every time I was asked a question I'd ask another question back. For instance, one man named Groff had state-of-the-art models of the newest electronic typewriter, and he was sure there was a big market for them in the Soviet Union. "Look, Harry, it would be a real contribution to the U.S. economy, maybe even foreign policy, if we could get a toehold. Where do I start?" "Well, Bert, have you ever worked with the government before?" I'd learn if he had or hadn't, and then why and how. Eventually I was able to pin down exactly what he wanted. (His hunch was that demand for his machines would be powered by engineering research labs. He needed to know where they were and especially how to contact their managers. As a bonus he taught me the basic economics of business machines and gave me a detailed account of his squalid family problems.) After stretching the conversation out to its limit, I ended it by promising some useful material at a future meeting.

I asked Patrick to help, and he supplied a few names – contacts of his own who would be useful to anyone doing business behind the Iron Curtain. I began a crash course in East European industry at the American Cultural Center on Place de l'Odéon. I had to come up with enough to keep my business clients at least willing to go on seeing me – they were paying me for my time.

But I'd begun dreaming of something better: finding or inventing an item so irresistible that I could auction it at a premium in this seller's market I'd wandered into.

My man at Les Iles Marquises called me on Monday, April 23. I remember the date because it's my daughter's birthday. (She was then living in Bali, where she'd had a daughter of her own two years before.) The headwaiter was pretty sure of his results. I could judge for myself by getting a copy of *Les Lauriers du lac de Constance*; there was a photograph of the author on the cover.

In ten minutes I had reached La Hune, the big bookstore at Saint Germain-des-Prés, and was holding the book in my hands. My brunette's name was Marie Chaix. In the little photograph on the back of the book she looked even more beautiful and aloof than when I'd seen her.

Her book was devastating. Marie had been born Marie-Claude Beugras, the daughter of a high-placed collaborationist. She had written a heartbreaking account of his life and her family's. They had all died, except for an older sister, Anne Sylvestre, a singer who happened to be performing that same month at the Théâtre des Capucines. I learned from friends that Marie had married a writer, Jean-François Chaix, and was living with him and their four-year-old daughter near Grimaud, a village back of Saint Tropez. She must be about fifteen years my junior.

I longed for her. I imagined her among silvery-gray olives and low-pruned vines, or in upper pastures where sheep had been wintering, full of thyme and rosemary and bordered with stands of holm oak. I couldn't go looking for her now; but there'd be other times.

THE MATERIAL I GAVE MY BUSINESS CLIENTS – THE NAMES OF Patrick's contacts and any relevant facts I'd picked up at the Cultural Center – was barely enough to keep them in tow. They obviously thought I was holding out on them. The one who knew Patrick told him that of course I was CIA: Locus Solus was the typical small-scale Company proprietary.

I told them that I was currently on the trail of an uncommonly valuable property. I was vague about the form it would take but clear about what it would reveal: the geographical disposition of the Soviet nuclear industry in central Siberia. I assured them there was no way to retrieve this information from official documents, no matter how cleverly you scanned them, or from any CIA working papers. (I made that part up.) It might take a couple of months, but when I laid my hands on what I was looking for, they would be the first to know. Each said that for that kind of scoop he was willing to wait.

A few days after reading Marie Chaix, I hatched a scheme.

For years I'd been a lover of Oriental rugs. Once I'd learned something about the subject, I realized the few pile rugs I'd already bought were third-rate. I settled for acquiring flatweaves (kilims); but even if I couldn't afford the true rugs I liked, I went on teaching myself about them. I did this not only by reading but by regularly visiting a right-bank shop on Rue Miromesnil. It was run by a father-and-son team named Shapazian. They were willing to educate me because I'd been introduced to them by one of their oldest clients; and I think they expected that some day they would manage to sell me something. So whenever one or the other had time to spare, he would talk to me about their store of tribal rugs, which were what attracted me most.

These sessions took place in the storeroom on the far side of the courtyard behind their shop. The room was twenty feet wide and fifty deep, filled to the ceiling with rolled or folded rugs that were stacked on the floor or on freestanding shelves. When you entered the room, you had to pass through a curtain of steel bars by way of a massive gate that was never left unlocked. Just behind the bars, a silent woman of Asian mien sat at a table in the righthand corner, with the rug she was currently restoring in front of her. She kept right on with her work when we came in and while the Shapazian of the day displayed some Caucasian or Turkman marvel for my benefit, pointing out peculiar distributions of cochineal and other subtleties.

My plan was to hire this woman. She would make the prize I'd sell to my American customers.

Plishkin was my inspiration. First of all, his situation was noble and dramatic: he was a genius battling a totalitarian regime that had thwarted his scientist's right to share the results of his research. One could imagine him fighting back with weapons of his own. He had access to politically sensitive information that could undermine the Soviets' obsession with secrecy and demonstrate his own personal power. For instance, he might reveal the locations of the factories, laboratories, and communications systems that formed the Siberian energy complex. It was a conceivable venture; and if Plishkin had embarked on it, his most effective tool would be a map.

Plishkin's map: that was what I would put up for sale. Of course it would be pure fiction. But this didn't really matter. Everyone was aware that Soviet maps were carefully distorted; no outsiders knew much about the actual topography of the relevant Siberian regions; so my map could represent almost any configuration and still appear plausible. Only one thing counted: it had to look like a map.

I already had a fictitious but genuine map at hand: a copy I'd made of the *Carte du tendre*, a classic French work that represents an imaginary Country of Love geographically. I'd already used a detail from the map in my third novel (see *Paris Review* 54, page 54), and I could reuse it now in more elaborate form. There was no chance of anyone recognizing it, especially if my new map were incorporated into a traditional carpet pattern. Patrick had told me Plishkin was being held in Khadistan. The Khadis are famous as weavers, known particularly for their original way of combining elements of Caucasian and North Afghan imagery. It might well occur to Plishkin to smuggle out his map by having it woven into a local rug.

I looked up a photograph of a Khadi saddle blanket. Its design was basically that of a modified "dragon" carpet , and I traced it onto a large sheet of paper. I divided my map into sections and copied them into the spaces surrounding the pattern. Finally I added the field ornaments typical of that style – tiny cypress trees – and filled in the border with traditional motifs. I drew everything in black except for the actual map. For that I used red and blue – these were the only obligatory colors; the weaver was free to decide about the rest.

I called at the Shapazian Gallery on the afternoon of May 2. The father was there, he had no customers to attend to, and he agreed to continue my lessons in carpetry. He locked the front door and took me back into the storeroom. Half an hour later we heard the phone ring out in front. Shapazian *père* went off to answer it. I knew it was Patrick calling. He'd promised to keep talking for at least ten minutes.

"*Madame*." She put down her work and slowly stood up. She turned towards me with her hands folded at her waist and bowed her head ever so little. Her expression was usually placid; now a lovely smile brightened up her face. She had large, liquid brown eyes and high cheekbones. Her nose and chin were delicate. She'd drawn her mass of brown hair into a neat coil behind her head. She was a big strong woman.

Could she weave me a rug according to a design I'd made? I unfolded my drawing. For a moment she went on staring into my eyes before looking at it. I told her the arrangement of red and blue lines had to be followed exactly.

She told me that with her job and a family to look after, a rug would take months. Did it have to be a rug? Her grandmother had taught her shawl-weaving – what about a shawl? It could be a large one – say two meters long and one wide. She'd need only a few weeks for that.

I agreed that that was a very good idea. (It would have suited Plishkin, too.) How much would she charge? She looked at me again, laughed, and said, "A dinner at Maxim's. With you."

"Are you sure? May I ask you what your name is?"

"Rkia." I tried pronouncing it a few times. "Never mind. My French friends, even my husband, everyone calls me – "

"Marie-Claude?" I ventured.

"Jo."

I wrote my own name and phone number for her on the back of the drawing. When I asked for her number, she shook her head. I could always reach her here. I was busy inspecting a Kazak rug when Shapazian reappeared.

She phoned next day. The design was more complicated than she'd thought. Doing it properly would take her at least six weeks. I could live with that.

I HAD NO PLANS FOR THE IMMEDIATE FUTURE. I THOUGHT OF going back to the U.S. to follow the Watergate hearings live – John Mitchell had admitted knowing about the break-in, so now the whole administration was in trouble, and having the Pentagon Papers case dismissed hadn't added to its luster. But I didn't want to give up my new life. Locus Solus had brought Patrick, Marie-Claude Quintelpreaux, and even business customers into my life. I was in a mood for more surprises. So I looked around for things to do while Jo wove my map.

I had dinner one evening that week at Maurice Roche's and Violante do Canto's apartment on Rue Berthollet. As usual, we drank ourselves silly – that is, Maurice and I did; after getting us fed, the lovely and devoted Violante quietly retired to her office and left us jabbering away happily by ourselves. Maurice did most of the talking, which wasn't a problem for me until, after we'd downed a dozen late-evening Scotches and the conversation inevitably turned to politics, he lost his temper and began attacking me. I'm not sure what, if anything, set him off.

"Harry, you're the ultimate asshole (*le dernier des cons*) – you and your whole fucked-up gang (*ta bande d'enculés*). You spend millions of dollars snooping around this country, and what do you know about the PCF?" *Le PCF*, or simply *le Parti*, meant *le Parti Communiste Français*, still the largest in France. "Fucking nothing (*foutre rien*). You've been told it's out to wreck your policy, and that's all you need to know. But things are a little more complicated. The Party's been around for fifty years. It has other traditions. It's full of fantastic men and women. You could at least take a look – you of all people."

I wasn't going to argue – any argument would have lasted till dawn, or my collapse; and anyway I agreed with him. Getting to know and understand the PCF, instead of just looking for confirmations of what was expected – wasn't that what at least some CI agents should be doing? Maybe some were. But I was myself as ignorant about the Party as Maurice had said. I realized how fascinating it would be it to learn more about it; and if things went badly, after all, what could a would-be agent ask for better than to be exposed and denounced by honest-to-God Communists?

That Sunday I walked down Boulevard Saint Germain and turned right up Rue Monge. Long ago the neighborhood had been the heart of the old student quarter, now it was modestly residential. I'd started out late in the morning. It was a warm day, with not many people around. It took me ten minutes to find what I was looking for: a young man carrying a large white shoulder-bag with *Humanité Dimanche* printed on it in large lettering. He was one of the volunteers the Communist Party sends out each week to peddle the Sunday edition of its paper. They work door to door and floor to floor. I stopped him between two small apartment buildings. I bought a paper and asked him if he could spare me a minute or two. I said I only wanted to talk to him about party business, now or later, whichever he preferred. He said he'd sold almost all his copies; now would be all right.

I identified myself as an American writer who'd lived in France for twenty years. Two important points: one, I'd been dead set against the Vietnam war ever since it started; two, I had good friends in the diplomatic corps and the international business community, and thanks to them I'd picked up a plethora of information about the war – information that had never been made known to the public.

I knew the French Communist Party had always resolutely opposed the U.S. intervention, and what I wanted to do now was communicate what I'd learned to rank-and-file party members. I'd spoken to several Communist intellectuals without much success, except for one woman. She said: forget about intellectuals, get the word out to the guys that matter. I asked her how, and what she suggested was what I was doing now. So would the young man speak to his comrades about me? I had friends in the Party who'd vouch for me. I mentioned Maurice Roche and Bruno Marcenac, the son of a well-known Communist poet. I insisted that I wanted no involvement with the Party beyond contributing what I knew about the war.

The young man's name was Jean-Louis. He knew who Jean Marcenac was. He said one thing he could do was relay my request to the person he was about to meet to settle the day's accounts. We agreed to meet in half an hour on Place de la Contrescarpe. Jean-Louis promptly disappeared into the next building.

He'd written down my name and references. If Bruno and Maurice were asked about me, they were bound to tell others what I was doing, and that would be a plus, even if nothing more came of the plan.

Of course I wanted more. I'd learned that the biggest excitement of subterfuge is getting other people involved. Other people brought an almost carnal scratch to the itch of my inflamed imagination.

On Place de la Contrescarpe I sat down in a bistro and had a dozen oysters and two glasses of Muscadet. Jean-Louis showed up looking glum. "Doing accounts with those guys is rough. One franc off and they take it out of your pocket. I delivered your message. He said, 'Tell the next cell meeting about it.' That'll be on Thursday."

I bought him a beer and *un hot-dog* and told him not to worry on my account. If they wanted to hear what I had to say, fine; if not, *tant pis pour eux!*

We had a patch of rainy weather, the off-and-on kind. True Parisians always seem to know when the changes are due. I look out one minute on sunny Rue de Varenne: not a raincoat or umbrella in sight. Ten minutes later it's pouring and everyone's in rain gear. Rain or shine, I kept my umbrella with me.

Wednesday I went with Patrick to Salle Gaveau where Michelangeli was playing Haydn and Mozart with the Ensemble Instrumental de France (an excellent band, and elegant, too – they performed standing in a semicircle around the piano). I told Patrick about my new project.

Jean-Louis called me Friday morning. His comrades had scheduled a "meeting under the trees" for me on Sunday in Parc Montsouris. He said this was a Party custom. I'd meet several members and lay out my case. He thought it was a good sign: "*Les réunions sous les arbres, c'est toujours sympa.*"

I hadn't expected the PCF to be so approachable. I started working on my Vietnam presentation, but it rained through the day and I got sleepier and sleepier and didn't make much progress. The rain stopped late in the afternoon. I decided to walk to the Galerie Flinker for Paul Jenkins's opening. (Paul made abstractions by pouring pools of paint onto the canvas, which he knew how to tilt back and forth to form designs he could control with deadly accuracy.) I saw several artists I knew: Shirley Jaffe, Shirley Goldfarb and Gregory Mazurovsky, Louis and Zuka Mittelberg, Kimber and Gaby Smith. Nobody was free for dinner and there weren't any single women to inveigle, so I walked around the corner for a quick meal alone at Le Muniche and then went home.

I consoled myself with the thought that if I was going to spend all next day concocting my Vietnamese revelations, this was the reasonable thing to do.

I needn't have gone to the trouble. Late Sunday morning I found seven people waiting for me at the lower end of Parc Montsouris, five men and two women. The sun was out, and everyone was friendly. Naturally they asked me questions, mainly a man the others referred to as "the superior." Most of the questions were about my personal life. I think they wanted to make sure I was on the level, that I was *sérieux*, and not some kind of nut or troublemaker. I acted very *sérieux*. I gave them names of respectable French friends. To explain how I'd come by my information, I recited lists of diplomats (which I made up – I wasn't going to involve Fred Warner) and businessmen (which I also made up, except for Frank Canfield, a friend of my parents who was running Esso's operations in Europe). I gave a prepared speechlet about why I wanted to speak to ordinary Party members – the progressive elements of our two countries should communicate directly, and so forth. They looked pleased.

They conferred. When they'd finished, the superior said that at that week's cell meeting they'd see what could be arranged, and we'd get together here again next Sunday. We all shook hands and started to go our separate ways. I asked the superior if I could have a word with him. I thanked him for giving me a hearing and invited him for lunch– there was an open-air restaurant on the far side of the park called the Pavillon du Lac. He was surprised; *I* was surprised when he accepted. He said he could use a break. He'd hardly paused since the end of the parliamentary election campaign.

He told me all about it over our meal. He'd done his work well, it had been a spectacular success; and it hadn't changed a damn thing.

It stayed sunny most of the week. I started going out on short walks – I'd wander around the gardens of the Musée Rodin or windowshop my way to the Seine past displays of stylish antiquities. Then King Faisal came on a state visit and turned my neighborhood into siren-land. I went to movies – *Sleuth*, *Travels with My Aunt*, *Othon*. (With Paris's movie madness and Lex Barker's death the week before, I expected a Tarzan festival any day.) I invented a few tropes for the next Oulipo meeting. Georges Perec gave them a weary nod over a late dinner at Le Balzar. I'd brought along the *Paris Review* with my translations of *Un homme qui dort*, the novel he was making his movie from. That perked him up.

The second meeting under the trees didn't last long. I met the cell secretary. I was being invited to speak to a meeting of sympathizers the coming Friday. Sympathizers, not members? There'd be members, too, himself included, and what was wrong with sympathizers? I thanked the cell secretary, and showed him, in the same *Paris Review*, my translation of Maurice Roche, a fellow Communist. He was polite about it.

Louise Dieudonné was there that Sunday. I'd known her in May, '68; we'd spent a night standing guard at the Writers Union. She was pretty and delicate, maybe twenty-eight years old at the time. When dawn came, I saw what had looked like a shadow on her left cheek turn into a three-inch-long red weal where a riot cop had slapped her with his gloved hand. Later we'd slept in each other's arms. I hadn't seen her since. She gave me a warm hug. What about lunch? No. Dinner? No, I mustn't insist.

I didn't. Before, she'd been alone; and unlike me, she wasn't the cheating kind.

Carlo Emilio Gadda, the uncrowned king of Italian letters, died the next day. Wednesday I went to a recital by Thierry de Brunhoff but couldn't get in. I had no TV, so Thursday evening I walked over to Henry and Judy Pillsbury's to watch an interview with Patrick Modiano, an interesting new novelist (the program was called *Apprendre à mentir* – Learning to Lie). And the evening after that I gave my talk.

I met Jean-Louis outside a café on Rue Saint-Jacques, just above Rue Soufflot. He took me through the café to a large room in back. On the way we passed a man sitting at a table between the window and the counter. He stared hard at me. He was thickset and impassive, with shoulder-length black hair. I'd seen him before – years before. Jean-Louis said, "Our Lambertiste spy." "Lambertiste?" "They're a Trotskyite minigroup. He's a total pain."

There were maybe twenty men and women in the back room; five or six more came in after we did. There were a few very young people, most were in their thirties or older. Everyone plainly dressed.

The cell secretary introduced me: American writer living in France, earns his living in a travel agency, long-time devotee of progressive causes. The atmosphere was good – no applause but nods of approval. The only problem was the light; all of it came from a few dim ceiling globes. I could hardly see my notes.

The gist of my "revelations" was: two big commercial enterprises were flourishing in Indochina, both of them illegal. One was an organized trade in opium from northern Laos (the crop was cultivated by the Hmong, called Méo by the French, a hill people allied to the United States). The other was the exploitation of high-grade uranium from a deposit located between northern Laotian towns of Luang Prabang and Phongsali and the North Vietnamese border. CIA ran the opium business, which financed and served as cover for the extraction of uranium ore and its transport south; several large private corporations were responsible for exporting it. The secret reason the U.S. air force had gone on bombing North Vietnam and Laos after the truce now became obvious: we were maintaining access for special forces to the mining area.

I'd just started telling my tale when a young woman stood up: "Monsieur, what you are saying is interesting. We all are grateful for the pains you have taken. But the revolution in Vietnam is almost complete. There is no longer an American presence there of any importance. For my friends and comrades here there have been other events in America that leave us perplexed. Could you consent to modify your topic for the evening and help us understand what you call *le ouateurguète* ?"

I thought, why not? "Very well. But I must first of all point out that to fully understand Watergate you must grasp the consequences of the situation I was describing just now. Because one must ask oneself, where was that uranium going? What was it to be used for?"

She stared at me blankly. "You are going too fast. I'm talking about something obvious. Why are these events being allowed to threaten the stability of the American government? Why are its ministers liable to go to prison? France after all is far more democratic than the United States, and here such things happen all the time. They have always happened. Every government spies on its opposition – ask the comrades here – and every government systematically denies it. It's part of the game. People usually laugh about such things, they don't hold solemn hearings to investigate them. We cannot imagine why you are all taking it so seriously."

"I see." She was making things easy for me – this was a subject that could be made to last as long as I liked; I'd already been through it several times with French friends who couldn't fathom Watergate either. So we discussed differences between American and French concepts of the state, of the authority of the executive, of the Official Lie. Because of my audience, I periodically added references to the corporate domination of public life – hardly news, but I gave it as sinister a slant as I could. There was a lot of arguing among members of the audience. This helped me look sober and well-informed, which I certainly wasn't.

When it was time to conclude, I tossed out a suggestion: some of the corporations exploiting the Laotian uranium I'd told them about had connections with the Republican Party, others had connections with the Democrats; it was the fierce competition between these corporations that lay behind the political crisis. I was rather pleased with this idea, which I'd improvised then and there. I hoped it wouldn't fall on deaf ears.

As I was leaving, the cell secretary took me aside. He congratulated me. He said that he and other Party members would try and organize an inter-cell meeting in the near future. That would give me a forum where I could go into my subject in depth.

I went out with Jean-Louis. The Lambertiste was right where we'd left him. Jean-Louis was carrying a shopping bag full of LPs. I asked, classical? jazz? pop? Not really. Recordings of his mother's political songs: "Political pop, I guess." His mother? Rosa Laporte. I vaguely knew the name – she was featured regularly at Party shindigs. But I knew the woman in the liner photograph more than vaguely: it was Jeannine Canson. I realized I'd known Jean-Louis, too, when he was a boy of five.

Jeannine was married to another Party stalwart, a painter who'd had some success producing domesticated Picassos. In the mid '50s Jean-Louis had been friends in kindergarten with my daughter. I picked her up one afternoon at their place off Rue Didot in the 14th arrondissement, an elegant street-level apartment with a little garden. The big living room opening on the garden had originally been two rooms; one of them probably a second bedroom, I thought, after Jean-Louis showed me where he slept – a kind of closet, with no window and no room for anything but his bed and a few shelves. Apparently he liked it, but I was horrified, and I blamed Jeannine for keeping her little son cooped up so they could look grand. Her husband was a gentle, modest man; she was intensely ambitious, both socially and intellectually. She was also attractive and very chic. That unsettled me. She was onto me in no time. She got me into her bed and after a few weeks got me out of it, all as amiably as can be. I had only fond memories of her as a lover.

I said nothing about any of this to Jean-Louis.

The next morning I was on my way out to see the Ad Reinhardt show at the Grand Palais when the cell secretary called: my inter-cell meeting was scheduled for 6 p.m. on Monday. That was only two days off. After my last experience with the Party faithful, I decided to wing it.

I spent Sunday afternoon with Marie-Claude Quintelpreaux – our third time together, during which we went on inching our way up the mountain of unconsummated desire (a desire visibly shared: uprightness and dewy glitter . . .). As usual we were naked and almost touching, this time miming nine positions from God knows what exotic Art of Love. Bathing the Lambs. The Brandished Lure. The Cool Proposal. The Roulade. The Night Bag. The Heirlooms. The Hand Passage. The Cantilever. The Spenserian Stance (this is my approximation of a structure in Sanskrit prosody). We held each pose for nine delirious minutes.

We'd barely started when Marie-Claude began making little growls and squeaks. She saw they were bothering me. She told me: "Do the same! Release the demons in you that molest pure yearning!" All right. There were demons – stupid wish lists, bits of nightmares to come. For a while the room sounded like a barnyard.

I begged her to let us finish. She sighed and shook her head. "The sensual being is like a child and must drink milk until ready for solid meat. Like those long in darkness, we must be content with the light of moon and stars until our eyes can endure the sun."

THE INTER-CELL MEETING ON MONDAY WASN'T THE RECEPTIVE forum I'd been promised. It was cordial enough, but over fifty members from the 5th, 6th, and 14th arrondissements had gathered in the local section offices on Square Adanson, off Rue Monge, and all of them apparently wanted their say. Every point I made led to questions and more questions, some of them totally irrelevant. For instance, an older woman wondered why our government was so hard on drugs when they were the perfect antidote to militant action. (I explained that FBI and CIA wanted drugs kept available so that left-wing leaders could be arrested on narcotics charges.) So I didn't get far with my explanation of Watergate. I didn't mind, even if I felt my talent for fiction was being wasted..

On my way out I ran into Jeannine Canson. She'd come to pick up her son, she said, and she was "so surprised" to see me! My foot.

"*Mon petit Harry*, I'm so happy to find you again. And tonight of all nights. Listen: they're throwing a fantastic party at a country club outside Paris. And you're coming with me." She didn't even let me say goodbye to my Party sponsors. And what about Jean-Louis? "He's a big boy now."

She'd parked her Mercedes on a nearby pedestrian crossing. I pointed out that I couldn't go to a party in the clothes I had on.

"We'll stop at your place. Still Porte de Vanves?"

"Rue de Varenne, off Rue du Bac. Number 35."

"*Je vois. Monsieur s'embourgeoise.*" She should talk.

Outside my building she left the car conspicuously straddling the curb on a block that was strictly no-parking. We went up to my apartment on the second floor. The place was small and low-ceilinged, with carpets and curtains of dark red and green and what is called discreet lighting. "A perfect love-nest!" That *was* the idea. I took the clothes I needed into the tiny office, then quickly washed in the bathroom next to it. There was a tap on the door as I was toweling myself dry. "May I?" She came in before I could answer. She looked me over. "Bravo. Svelte as ever. Too bad about your hair. But women don't really mind about that." She ran her fingers through the curls I had left. I wishfully interpreted this as an invitation and reached out for her. "Are you crazy? This make-up is the work of a master. Later. Maybe."

I put on my fancy maroon velvet suit; Jeannine insisted on picking out my tie. We drove out of town in German comfort – and what did the Party faithful think of her ritzy ways? I was still such a child! She was *working* for the Party tonight, and it wasn't an occasion for gnarled hands and overalls. Hyundai, the South Korean *chaebol*, was setting up in France and had thrown this party to celebrate. Chung Ju Ying, the founder, would be there, along with significant relatives and bigwigs. Four PCF members had been assigned to get a message across to the Koreans: whatever they planned to go into – shipbuilding, construction, manufacturing upscale machinery – good labor relations meant dealing directly with the CGT, the biggest union in the country and Party-controlled). South Korean entrepreneurs might hate Communists, but they were businessmen. The more reassuring the image Jeannine and her colleagues projected, the easier their task would be.

"You mean the Party's paying for your make-up job and the Mercedes?" Not the Party itself: its Soviet friends kept a slush fund for all kinds of expenses. "Just what your people do for the Socialists." She didn't know the details. Once, she'd heard, Siberian furs were exported to Belgium and the proceeds moved to offshore accounts held by Party sympathizers, who then footed the bills.

We were past Fontainebleau. We turned off the autoroute, drove through Moret-sur-Loing, and soon came to the country club. There was a Louis XIII manor house at its center; the outlying buildings were neo-Art Nouveau. A pastoral effect was supplied by a golf course stretching into the dusk.

Jeannine got off at the clubhouse entrance. No valet service in sight, so I left the Mercedes in a nearby field. A couple of hundred cars were already parked there, with more arriving. A lot of black official cars, with chauffeurs standing around them smoking and swapping jokes. On my way back I spotted Patrick on the other side of the parking lot. I waved to him, but he turned and disappeared.

I dropped the car keys at the entrance as I'd been told to do and gave my name. While they were checking it, someone brushed against me. I looked around and saw an older blonde woman hurry off. I found a folded card in my side jacket pocket, with a few scribbled words:

You don't know me

Suor Angelica

Seeing Patrick here was no surprise – Hyundai manufactured offshore equipment. But why would he want to avoid me? Of course I'd play along.

I spotted the blonde woman standing at a nearby outdoor bar. She was speaking to the barman, not drinking anything. I walked over and stood next to her, hoping to learn something. She gave me a single cursory glance before walking away.

I drank four glasses of champagne. They did me good, after the long inter-cell meeting and my non-stop abduction. I couldn't see Jeannine anywhere.

A stranger accosted me, a tall blondish man in his forties. He was a ringer for Elliott Ness as played by Robert Stack.

"Alone?" he asked, with a big smile. I said I was waiting for a friend.

He paid no attention. "An man alone and an second man alone – bad! Let us unify." He certainly didn't talk like Elliott Ness. His accent was coarse and obscure. His face was set in a hallucinatory grin.

I saw Jeannine not far off and waved. She was staring vaguely in my direction. A thin older man in a cut-rate dark blue suit was addressing her intently. When she turned away, she was visibly upset.

"I am Mitchell," my intruder announced, clapping a large, strong hand on my shoulder. *Mitchell?* I told myself, a sozzled hanger-on. He moved his hand to my arm and started firmly leading me away from the bar towards the far end of the clubhouse. It seemed as though I were walking two feet above the ground. Wine didn't usually affect me that way.

From somewhere in the crowd on the lawn voices were noisily raised. A few tough young Koreans appeared out of nowhere. Mitchell kept me moving. "Behind corner – behind *an* corner," he corrected himself, "we can amuse." Did that mean sexual assault? A place to smoke a joint? I concentrated on walking soberly. The grass was turning greener by the second.

Round the corner there was a flat space overlooking the eighteenth green. Part of it was marked off in a long, narrow rectangle, now spotlighted. At either end a steel peg was set in a sunken square box filled with mucky clay. No grass between the boxes, just trampled dirt.

We stopped at a rack fixed to the clubhouse wall. It was hung with quoits of rope and steel. Mitchell handed me a steel one.

Had I ever played quoits? Wasn't it a steamship game? I'd been pretty good at horseshoes.

We took off our jackets. Mitchell motioned me to start. I made five ringers straight off and had another streak at my next turn. I didn't give a damn what I was doing. Mitchell's quoits all banged off the unyielding pins. The sound was deafening. It was as if the quoits were made of rubber and the clangs were clumsy offstage dubbing.

After a while Mitchell gave up. "Big unluck." He buttoned his shirtsleeves and picked up his jacket. "Come now. I show you an sight."

We set off down the return leg of the fairway. It was a mess – unreplaced divots everywhere, as though a charter-tour of duffers had played over it. The holes magically disappeared as we approached them. A trick of twilight?

At the fifteenth green we waded through a wide expanse of rough until we came to another green, one nearer the start of the course. Below its sloping sides lay a small pond. Its surface was black and glassy.

"An little area, an great deep. Maybe two hundred meter. Too: not empty! An beast below. People tell, an golfman pass, beast out! Attack!"

"Any supporting evidence?" I asked. "Like photographs?" Darkness settled over us. At the center of the pond I saw a momentary heaving of the black water. I turned away and leaned on Mitchell's shoulder.

"An thing wrong?"

We started back. At the first tee a television team had set up floodlights and was filming guests as they took practice drives. When we went by, Jacques Brel was the driver. I stopped for a closer look. This wasn't possible. It wasn't real.

I watched the singer prepare and deliver his swing as each new ball was set up for him. He did this again and again. His gestures never varied. He wasn't real. His plastic skin and clothes gleamed with slick light. Solid golf balls shot off into the night.

Mitchell was checking his watch. "An time come." He led me to the manor house door and left me there. I went in and ate six leftover canapés. There was a bar; I had more champagne. No sign of Jeannine.

The bar was in the central room of the building, which I took to be the former ballroom. It had a high frescoed ceiling, three monumental chandeliers, and walls stuccoed *à la vénitienne*. In each of the ceiling's corners there were dark flutterings. These crystalized into bevies of grackles fastened to the angles by invisible threads, beating their wings and barking distantly. I didn't take a second look.

A young man came up and spoke to me softly: "Monsieur Mathews? Madame Canson was obliged to go back to Paris. I am to drive you home."

I had just ordered another glass of champagne. Would he care to join me?

"I had better not. But I shall sit with you." He paused. "I have been asked to tell you something. The evening did not go as planned."

"I'll say."

"What happened to you was part of it. I'm not sure of the details, but basically, influential right-wing people found out we would be here. They brought in a gang of heavies, eastern European types. We could not approach the people we wanted to talk to. We were physically threatened. So Madame Canson and the others decided to leave. Meanwhile you had been taken far away from the scene." He paused. "We are convinced that your first drinks were drugged."

I laughed. "*That's* a relief. It explains those fucking birds."

"Birds?"

"I was seeing live birds in the corners of the ceiling here." I looked up. "I *still* see them."

"Be reassured, please – they are there. It is a Korean practice. The birds are symbols of the Spirit of Enterprise struggling to break free. At midnight the birds will be cut loose as a signal of forthcoming prosperity."

"But *grackles*?"

"I feel the same way about capitalists. It is not a bad match."

We started off towards the parking area. Patrick and Mitchell were chatting at a table on the lawn. They didn't notice me.

Two days later the cell secretary called and told me I'd been invited to address a section meeting (the section was the next highest Party unit). I accepted because I'd been treated so well, but that would be it. My involvement with the PCF had gone far enough. I never heard from Jeannine.

THE WEATHER STAYED WARM. U.S. NEWSPAPERS NOW HAD Watergate all over their front pages. The Dow fell below 900 again. The really bad news came from Chile – a decent country was being systematically crippled. The Cannes film festival ended. Jackie Stewart won the Monaco Grand Prix and tied Jimmy Clark's record for victories. At our May meeting, several first-generation Oulipians blamed newer members for taking the group too seriously and spoiling their fun. On Sunday, June 3, a supersonic Tupolev-144 flown in for the Le Bourget air show crashed in Goussainville, killing six people besides its crew.

On June 4 Maurice Roche phoned: he knew I was giving a talk at a Communist meeting next day and warned me there might be trouble.

The crowded room I walked into on Square Adanson was abnormally quiet. I saw the cell secretary on the podium with his colleagues and nodded to him. A portly, sour-faced man I'd never seen was sitting in the center of their row. As I came through the door he held up a hand to stop me. "Monsieur Matiouze," doing his best to make the name sound silly, "Monsieur Matiouze, we have been waiting for you."

"Who are you, monsieur?"

"It is no business of yours. Now you are going to listen to what I have to say." His tone was contemptuous, which brought some disapproving mumbles from the audience. "Comrades, you too must listen. I know you have had a good time with Monsieur Matiouze. We are not here to have a good time. The purpose of Party meetings is not entertainment. The purpose of Party meetings is to strengthen and support the French working class. Monsieur Matiouze is no friend of the French working class. In fact Monsieur Matiouze can be considered to be objectively an enemy of the working class and so of the Party that represents it. You see, he belongs to an organization radically opposed to our interests."

It was too good to be true. What I'd dreaded so often was about to happen again, only now it was as if my highest wish was being granted. The French Communist Party was about to identify me officially as an American agent. It was, as they say, publicity money can't buy. The sour-faced man continued:

"Monsieur Matiouze is a member of something called the Ouvroir de Littérature Potentielle, or Oulipo. The Oulipo is a gang of cynical formalists. They claim to be materialists, but they utterly disregard the dialectic of history. Their materialism is nothing but a degraded manifestation of bourgeois idealism. Naturally the Oulipo is opposed to any kind of literature that puts itself at the service of historical progress, especially socialist realism. No Oulipian, and certainly not an American one, is a man whose opinions are worth listening to. Monsieur Matiouze, you are informed that you will no longer be welcome among us."

In the audience Louise Dieudonné stood up and asked to speak. She was told to sit down.

I felt utterly deflated. Instead of being conspicuously branded as CIA, I'd been relegated to a tiny niche that few people had heard of and that was generally thought to be downright silly. I managed to work up a semblance of *hauteur* and said, "I regret the Communists in the Oulipo are not here to correct you. Friends, many thanks for your welcome."

"Bonsoir, Monsieur Matiouze."

The superior joined me outside: "That's too bad. I don't see what the problem is. How about a drink?" We set out for the café across Rue Monge. The Lambertiste was there sitting alone at a terrace table. It was then that I remembered where I'd seen him first.

It was in May, '68, the evening when De Gaulle made a discouraged speech that left us all sure his days in power were numbered (and they were, but otherwise). There was a big demo on Boulevard Sebastopol. At sunset the riot police started charging the demonstrators from the northern end of the boulevard. That was when my Lambertiste appeared – in those days he would have belonged either to the Trotskyist OCI or its ally, the AJI. He was one of the youths who confidently moved out of the crowd and headed for the "front line." They were stocky and ready for rough stuff, with gloves and boots and bandanas under their chins to pull up when the tear gas started. They were warriors in our good cause. The rough stuff that night was very rough. I luckily found my daughter and hustled her out of there.

Here he was five years later. Did he spend all his time watching his eternal "Stalinist" adversaries and reporting to Pierre Lambert? Did he want to remind them by his presence that some day they would be judged in the court of International Communism? As I sat drinking with the superior, I then thought: maybe he's on his own. Maybe he's play-acting, like me – someone who'd been stuck with a reputation and decided to go with it. When I left, I looked at him with new interest. We were all after some kind of happiness, and this leftist heavy might have found his. He gave me a cool stare back.

I had no more Party meetings to go to; but there were plenty of other entertainments in Paris that June. Paul Taylor and his company were at the Théâtre de la Ville. Movies that had first screened in Cannes were being shown commercially. *La Grande Bouffe* was the one people talked about – too black for some tastes, but everyone agreed to adore Andréa Ferréol. Another Oulipo meeting was coming up. I think the only item I prepared was an account of our public blacklisting by the Communists.

Early in the month I received a letter from the USSR Tourist Department, delivered by hand. I knew the Tourist Department was in reality the KGB's 2nd Directorate, specializing in counterintelligence work among Americans and Brits visiting the Soviet Union.

The letter requested that I come to their offices a week later. It read more like a summons than an invitation. It included a cozy threat: "Your firm, Locus Solus, is not properly registered in this country. This is not our concern, but we look forward to your explaining your activities as its representative." I hadn't any qualms about Locus Solus's legal status. It wasn't only unregistered, it was technically nonexistent. Anyway, I was glad to be getting inside the Soviet Embassy, which happened to be only a block away on Rue de Grenelle.

At 9 A.M. on Wednesday, June 13, I showed up at the embassy gate with my passport and the official letter. I was checked at the gate, again at a booth on the embassy steps, and finally at a counter inside. A guard took me across a rear courtyard to the back of the building and into a little waiting room.

Two men were sitting there leafing through Soviet illustrated magazines. One of them said hello and hoped I wasn't in a rush

– they'd been there since 8. Both were wearing western clothes that didn't look quite right. They spoke French with a slight and charming accent. They acted pleased to have someone else to talk to and started complaining about Soviet bureaucrats – this wasn't their first time here and probably wouldn't be their last – and almost casually asked what my own business was. I said I didn't know – the Tourist Department had requested I come in, but perhaps it had heard I was planning to go to the Soviet Union for the first time. Then I launched into a non-stop panegyric on Russian culture – the wonders of Biely and Blok, Balakireff and Prokofiev. They were very uninterested.

My name was called. I exited the room by a back door that had quietly opened and found a blonde woman waiting for me. A buxom, stony-faced blonde, the kind of blonde a saint wouldn't look at in a stained-glass window. We followed a couple of dreary corridors to a small office – minimal furniture, artificial lighting. I was directed to a wooden chair facing a long bare desk covered in some kind of ersatz linoleum. On its far side was a chromed-metal armchair upholstered in puffy black plastic.

I waited for another quarter of an hour. A heavyset man came in and sat down behind the desk. He had lank, straight white hair, pocked ruddy skin, blue eyes, broad cheekbones, a fleshy mouth. He was wearing a rumpled gray suit, white shirt, and brown tie. He nodded at me, placed several folders on the desk, and stared at me glumly. Then, in a surprisingly high-pitched voice and confident English:

"Mathews, why do you think you've been called in here?"

I kept my smile down. It was game time.

"That's not what I'd call a 'captation of pleasure,' Mr. . . . ? Colonel . . . ? Sergeant . . . ?"

"I ask you – "

"Your letter said I was 'urgently invited.' Is that the same thing as being 'called in'? Am I free to leave?"

"You might have some difficulty finding your way out. This will not take long. Again, why do you think you are here?"

"I guess my plans for visiting the Soviet Union – "

"A stupidity. Where were you during the hours preceding the sabotage of our Tupolev-144 at Le Bourget"

"Do I answer your questions or just listen? I know one of your people once said that if others talk, conversation becomes difficult – "

"Answer, please."

"That was Sunday, June 3? Actually, I was at the Georges V playing canasta with the Soviet ambassador's wife. Top floor. I forget the room number, but there were witnesses."

"The ambassador's wife was not in Paris at the time. Where were you?"

"That's who she *said* she was."

"We deduce that you were part of the plot –"

"Then tell the French police. It happened on their territory, not yours."

"Potsdam, however, is on the territory of one of our allies. What were you doing at the Potsdam bridge on December 31?"

"December 31?"

"There was an exchange of captured agents between the DDR and the western occupation forces."

"Then wouldn't I have been at the western end of the bridge? Anyway I was at a houseparty on the road from Paris to . . . Never mind."

"Who else was present at this houseparty?"

"Um, Giulio Andreotti . . . Mel Brooks . . . I think."

"You have also applied for a fellowship that will allow you to spend an entire year in Berlin. A so-called cultural fellowship. Will your cultural activities include helping colleagues of your 'dissident' Soviet friends to betray their country?"

"If my DAAD application is accepted, what I'll mainly do is work – I mean, write. Get to know the literary community. Visit museums, see the Berliner Ensemble, go to the opera. You must know I love opera. And I haven't met a single Soviet exile here or anywhere else."

"Wednesday, June 6, between 23 hours and midnight, you were drinking with a friend on the terrace of Le Select in Montparnasse. It is a well-known meeting-place for what you call exiles. Seven were seated at tables next to yours. You were thus observed consorting openly with renegades, not to use a harsher and better term."

"Colonel, you have the beauty of the clear of sight, but you are looking at a picture. If I were working against you, is this something I would do in public? Did I speak to any of my criminal neighbors? I wish I had. They were enjoying themselves."

"Mathews, you are stubborn as a toothache. I look not at one picture but a series of pictures, every one tells the same story, every one has you at the center. You could make things simpler by explaining what is already staring me in the face."

"I'm sorry, but I enjoy saying what I mean."

Another man had come in. He said, in a quiet voice, "Serguei, may I have a few moments with Monsieur Mathews?"

My inquisitor whispered a few words in Russian and left.

"Is it all right if we speak French?" the new man asked me. "It is much easier for me – I learned it from my reactionary grandparents." He smiled. "And I know you are fluent in it. My name is Vladimir. May I call you Harry, without disrespect? I so enjoy your custom of using first names right away."

Late thirties; his auburn hair, gray eyes, and thin features made him look more Anglo-Saxon than Slav. He wore tan linen slacks and a long-sleeved navy-blue polo shirt.

"I'm afraid Serguei speaks rather bluntly – his peasant's tongue. He was only doing his job. We do not want to interfere with your life. However, your activity does not conform to familiar patterns."

"My activity?"

"Harry, may I be frank and request that you in turn be frank with me? You were in Laos at a delicate moment during the Vietnamese war of independence. In May, 1968, you took an active role in the Writers Union, siding with its leftist, anticommunist faction. Recently, you insinuated yourself into meetings organized by the French Communist Party in order to disseminate false information. None of this, Harry, is especially disturbing. But there is one matter that perplexes us."

"My public proposals for a voyage through central Siberia?"

"Exactly."

"I tried to talk to your colleague about it. He brushed me off."

"He does things his way. I'm willing to address the subject."

"OK, Vladimir. But you won't be satisfied by what I say."

"I will be if you're frank with me. This is the point: advocating the journey you described cannot have been due to chance."

"Of course not."

"That journey is both provocative and impossible. Foreigners would not be allowed to set foot on some of the trains in your schedule."

"I proposed the itinerary deliberately, but not for reasons you imagine. The Siberian round trip was a way of demonstrating the kind of extended travel planning I wanted to encourage in my listeners. I was there to help them, after all."

"Forgive my scepticism. Merely raising the prospect of travel through that region is an incitement to subversion. We are convinced of that."

"It was not my intention. You yourself just said that making the trip is impossible."

"That's irrelevant. You were giving a signal of some kind – but to whom? That, my dear Harry, is what we have to know." (I felt like answering: everyone in Paris!)

"I was recently elected to the Oulipo – you know what that is?"

"I do."

"Can you understand that working out the Siberian itinerary – stitching its segments into a continuity – gave me enormous satisfaction as an Oulipian?"

"Is it the Oulipo that has made contact with Plishkin?"

"Plishkin! I'd never heard of him before."

"What exactly does the political activity of the Oulipo consist of?"

"Nothing. I think most of its members are leftish, but each goes his own way."

"Queneau collaborated with Bataille and Suvarin in their attacks on the Soviet Union."

"That was forty years ago. I have no idea what his views are now. There is no political discussion at our meetings. As far as I can tell, *nobody* in the Oulipo is politically active."

"Except you, dear Harry. Tell me, exactly how many travelers has Locus Solus counseled? Does Elzbieta Sosnowska exist?"

"Vladimir, we've had any number of clients. And I'll be damned if I'll give a Russian information about someone of Polish origin. I can at least assure you that she isn't living either in Paris or Lans-en-Vercors."

"The trouble with everything you've told me, Harry, indeed with everything you've done, is that the pieces don't fit. There is the mystery of your Siberian project, and I do wish you'd be more candid about that; and then the rest. The rest is so arbitrary and (please forgive me) so *amateurish*. Making chalk marks on walls! Can't you possibly tell me whom you're acting for? It can't conceivably be your government. Oh, one other question. What are your relations with Jeannine Canson?"

"Oh, that's easy enough to explain." I told him about my daughter's kindergarten friendship with Jean-Louis. "We happened to meet last month when I was 'disseminating false information' to the PCF. I don't know why she took me along to that crazy party. As for your other question – can you reasonably expect me to answer that, except to say that I haven't been 'acting' on behalf of anyone?"

"I'm disappointed in you, Harry. Thank you for your time." I was shown out.

I was barely through the embassy gate when I heard a familiar voice calling my name. I looked back and saw Patrick hurrying after me. I hadn't heard from him since the Hyundai bash. He looked concerned.

"What the hell were you doing in the lions' den? Are you all right?"

"Bright-eyed and bushy-tailed. I don't really know why they're so interested. I was going home to call you for an enlightened opinion. Lunch?"

"I can't. Don't miss the Perec review in *Le Monde.* Why don't you come and hear Pollini with me tomorrow night? Schoenberg, Webern, and two late Beeths. We can talk then."

We walked together as far as the kiosk on Boulevard Raspail. I noticed that the men we passed all looked unusually furious. "Has something happened I don't know about?"

"The government had made seat belts compulsory and set a 55 mile-an-hour speed limit on ordinary roads."

We said goodbye; I bought *Le Monde.* I decided that what I needed was a good meal in a calm place. I managed to land a table in the near-empty back room at Aux Fins Gourmets, a few doors away. The review of Georges's book, in which he recounted a year's worth of dreams, was noncommittal but left a definitely favorable impression. I was happy Georges was getting some attention. His career had been declining for a long time.

One thing I appreciated in Patrick was his love of music. That Thursday he listened intently to each work Pollini played (and we were given the whole "Les Adieux" sonata as an encore).

We ate afterwards. Patrick made me repeat every word Serguei and Vladimir had said to me. He told me I needn't worry. They'd never denounce me to the French. Either they'd decide I wasn't worth bothering about or they'd keep tabs on me to trace my connections. But, I asked, what did it all *mean*? Patrick said, not much of anything.

Jo had phoned me earlier. Her five-year-old daughter had come down with measles, and she had her hands full, especially now that the girl wouldn't be leaving for summer camp. She promised the shawl by mid July. Another month to wait.

I asked Patrick if he had any suggestions about how to fill the time. Didn't Zapata Petroleum need any documents delivered these days? What about a nice pick-up in Gstaad or Capri?

Patrick laughed. "We're not into that kind of thing. Not yet, anyway. Haven't you been managing to keep busy on your own?"

I told him my "infiltration" of the PCF had been terminated.

"It wasn't because of anything that happened at the Hyundai fiesta, was it?"

I was glad he'd finally brought it up. "What did happen? Why the cold shoulder?"

He'd been ashamed to tell me: he'd lost his nerve. He hadn't gone to the party to connect with Hyundai: he was only tagging along with a particular guest in the Soviet delegation. (Its mission was to sell the Koreans Siberian gas.) Patrick had recently been trying to get information about certain undeveloped Soviet oil fields and perhaps secure future access to them. For days he'd been courting a seedy top-level manager at Gazprom who was in Paris. He'd taken him out to lunch and dinner. He'd spent hours plying him with vodka and champagne in dreary Montmartre nightclubs. He'd provided classy overnight companions from Madame Claude's. Nothing worked.

What worked was an idea he'd had on the spur of the moment the night before the party. He started telling the manager Polish jokes, except that he replaced the Poles with Americans and swore that every story was true. Furthermore he gave his anecdotes grisly endings: the American idiot invariably ended up in prison, or hospitalized, or dead. The Russian enjoyed each story and asked for more; and next morning he gave Patrick his personal phone numbers, asked him to keep in touch, and typed up a letter of intent that was as close to an option as he was ever likely to see. Then they went off to the Hyundai evening together.

"I spent the whole time with those guys. When I saw you I thought, the last thing I need now is an amiable American friend. It was stupid. I could have managed."

"Fair enough. But you didn't have to tell that ding-dong alien to take me for a walk."

Patrick made no comment. He said he was leaving Paris next day on business. He'd be back at the end of the following week. I could leave a message with his secretary if I needed to reach him.

I DIDN'T HAVE TO RESORT TO A MESSAGE. I CAUGHT PATRICK THE following morning before he left. I needed his advice.

At 9 A.M. I'd received a call from someone I didn't know, a Frenchman who had been informed that I worked for an exceptional sort of travel agency and thought I might agree to provide a special service. He was not in need of travel counsel; he was looking for someone who could undertake a short trip on his behalf in order to convey a confidential dossier to a prospective client. The operation would benefit greatly from having an intermediary unassociated with any of the parties involved. Would I agree to act as this intermediary? My expenses would be generously covered and I would be well paid. The work should take no more than two or three days. I would not, he insisted, be running any kind of risk.

I asked why he had approached me in particular for this assignment. He replied that one of my "business associates" had recommended me as wholly reliable. But he refused to name the associate – he had promised him "discretion."

I requested time to think his offer over. Reasonable enough, he acknowedged, and gave me a phone number. I should inform him of my decision no later than 5 P.M.

I asked Patrick what he thought of the proposition.

"It's hard to say. There's not much in it for you, is there? Aside from the money – make sure you get all the details on that, and insist on being paid at least half up front. On the other hand, what have you got to lose? Since the guy got in touch through one of your business pals, it's probably some financial deal that has to be settled secretly before anyone goes public with it. I guess if you haven't got anything else to do and want to pick up a little tradecraft, you could give it a try. You'll probably learn a little more about dead drops and other basic routines. And who knows, maybe your contact on the other end will be a Hungarian dish. It's up to you."

Learning more about basic routines appealed to me. I called the Frenchman and told him I'd take on the job if the money was right. He quickly reassured me on that point, then began briefing me:

"You know the church at Saint Sulpice? Saturday the 23rd, around 4 P.M., a package will be deposited in the third confessional on the right on the penitent's seat. Go in at 4:30, spend some time looking at the Delacroix chapel, and have the package out of there by 5. You'll be able to fit it into a briefcase or a large shopping bag. Take a cab at the taxi stand on the square and have it drop you off on Rue de Bellechasse. Then walk straight home. You'll find instructions in the package. Got that? Please repeat everything back."

I did as I was told.

"Good. Don't forget a word of it. And don't write it down."

SATURDAY THE 23RD: THAT STILL LEFT OVER A WEEK WITH nothing to do.

I read in next day's *Le Monde* that Dr. Pierre Royer had been picked to run the top medical research center in France, the Institut Pasteur. Fifteen years before, he'd diagnosed and treated an undocumented kind of hypoglycemia that was giving my son severe convulsions. A good man was being rewarded.

In the same issue I learned that the police were reinforcing their protection of the Tupolev-144 that had crashed on June 3. That could only mean that pieces of the wreckage had been stolen – CIA work, perhaps? There was an opening for me here, a chance to try my hand peddling an intelligence item before I had my prize map to work with. And I knew where to find what I needed.

After our marriage had ended, my wife had taken up with our friend Jean Tinguely, a kinetic sculptor who had since then made a name for himself with his motor-driven constructions. He and Niki had settled in Soisy-sur-École, a village an hour south of Paris. They eventually married. Soon after that they began leading separate lives, but they remained close friends. I was on good terms with both of them.

Jean was an expert metal worker and a compulsive junk collector – junk was his primary raw material. I called him up and the next day I drove out to Soisy to see him. Jean's junk had become monumental: there was a flywheel fifteen feet across and several twenty-foot steel beams in his front yard.

Seppi, his assistant, let me in; Jean joined me on the back terrace for a glass of Saint Saphorin. I told him what I was looking for. He took me into a storeroom and showed me a jet engine hanging intact from the ceiling. "We can use it as a model. Which part were you thinking of?"

"A fuel injector? Too complicated, I guess. A piece of the compression chamber?"

"We can handle that. Better stay away. The sparks can burn holes in those pretty clothes." I sat on the terrace and enjoyed the summery view and listened to the sounds of metal being sawed and bashed. Jean came back: "We'll let it cool slowly the way it would have. It's real titanium. One of Shelby's engineers let me have a few of their scraps." Jean was a racing-car fanatic, and he'd made his way into its high circles. "Listen, for years I've been telling everyone you're *not* CIA. What's the deal?"

"It's a game I'm enjoying. There are even people who think I've got access to hot stuff – no point letting them down. Fifty-fifty, OK?"

Seppi wrapped a length of scorched and twisted metal in burlap and laid it in the trunk of my rental car. I eventually deposited it in my apartment, and I was wondering what to do next when I got a call from Groff, the electric-typewriter salesman. He wanted to know how long I was planning to keep him on the hook. Not much longer, I told him, and did he know anyone who might be interested in a portion of crashed Tupolev?

"For Christ's sake, not on the phone. Can you hold it till Monday?"

The weekend was coming up; people might be hard to reach. "Sure."

Life was definitely improving.

Groff showed up late Monday morning with another man. He wasn't introduced. I unpacked the piece of titanium in front of them. The other man tapped it with the butt of his pocket-knife and scraped it here and there. "Where'd you get it?"

"You know I can't tell you that."

"How do you know it's for real?"

"Because I know the man who made it," I said. "Look, it's a first-hand source. They've always been reliable."

"What's the price tag?"

"It's on consignment."

"So?"

"Two thousand."

"Francs?"

"No, *not* francs."

The man produced a stack of dollars and counted them out. We rewrapped the piece, and they left. I sat down and wrote Jean Tinguely a check for three thousand Swiss francs on my Geneva account.

I HAD ONE REGRET. I'D NEVER SOLD ANYTHING SUCCESSFULLY before, and now I'd jumped at the first offer instead of taking my time and contacting several buyers. I would have acquired more experience, and more money as well.

Marie-Claude Quintelpreaux wasn't answering the phone, not even by machine. I went to see Jo at the Shapazian Gallery. She wasn't there that day.

Thursday night I was on my way home from a late drink with Paul Taylor when I almost got caught in a riot: North Africans, police using tear gas, and gangs from Ordre Nouveau, which had held a meeting earlier in the Palais de la Mutualité. Its theme had been: Stop illegal immigration. In plain language, Get the Arabs out of France.

Saturday, June 23: chilly and overcast. I walked to Place Saint-Sulpice around 4 and had a coffee at the Café de la Mairie. I read in the paper that Pontus Hulten, someone who'd always supported Niki and Tinguely, was being appointed director of the new Centre Pompidou. At 4:30 I went across to the church carrying a big empty Arnys shopping bag. I spent a few minutes in the chapel with the Delacroix paintings, as instructed, then sat down in a central pew for a look around.

It seemed odd to have scheduled the pick-up for a Saturday afternoon. That's when confessionals are at their busiest. The third one on the right was empty, though. I walked up the center aisle, turned right in front of the high altar, and came back down the side aisle until I spotted the package. I swept it straight into my shopping bag and slunk out of the place.

I opened the package at home: two envelopes inside, a large manilla one sealed with tape and an ordinary business-size one marked "Courier." Inside was a typed itinerary, a roundtrip airplane ticket to Vienna, a roundtrip train ticket from Vienna to Graz, and small packets of francs and schillings. I had to get to Graz next day, register at the Hotel Drei Raben (Annenstrasse 43, phone 71 26 86), and wait there for "Cyrille" to call for the other envelope. He would arrive in a day or two.

I waited five days. My only interest in Graz was that the hero of Hofmannsthal's *Andreas* had hired his criminal manservant there at the beginning of his adventures. I never got to see the town – I didn't dare go out for more than twenty minutes. The hotel and its restaurant were "decent." The couple that ran them were smugly polite. Local customers spoke a German I could barely understand. I found a few books to read at a bookshop in the neighborhood.

When "Cyrille" finally appeared, he thanked me for the delivery and offered no apology for the delay. He said he'd like to buy me a drink, even dinner, but would that be prudent? "Permit me at least to introduce myself: Hubert Massol." I didn't react, so he added, "But you must know me."

I shook my head. "Monsieur, your name means nothing to me."

"Of course. That is much more reasonable."

I changed my ticket for the third time and was back in Paris July 1. I found an envelope slipped under my door. (How had they gotten into the building?) Compliments for my patience, the rest of my stipend, plus a thousand francs for extra expenses. I shouldn't call. He'd be in touch if he needed me again.

I STILL HAD TWO WEEKS TO WAIT. I USED THEM TO CLEAR UP Locus Solus business: even a trickle of requests can land you with a backlog. I referred routine inquiries to my own travel agents, a small, efficient place on Rue de Luynes that even gave me a percentage on their larger commissions. I put off nuts and bores by advising them to deal with Madame Sosnowska, who was never available. I kept for myself a few cases that appealed to me. One example:

An American couple had been occasional visitors to France for many years. They had seen the major tourist attractions; they now wanted to get to know the other France, *la France profonde*. They had bought a car for the purpose. They were retired and ready to devote whatever time was needed to their project.

I explained to them that the silent majority in France was Catholic by tradition and suggested that it might be appropriate for them to travel around the country by way of small towns that had been named after saints of the Roman church. I could prepare them a list of such towns that would be subdivided into clusters of four or five concentrated in each of the more interesting regions. By the time they'd finished, they'd know the country backwards and forwards.

My clients were intrigued by the idea, and I spent a day drawing up their itinerary. They would start near the center of France at Saint Agrève, then proceed through the southwest via Saint Bauzile, Saint Céré, Saint Denis-les-Martel, Saint Étienne-Cantalès, Saint Flour to Saint Gaudens; from there go on to the next region; and after circling the country, end in the west with stops in Saint Ursin, Saint Vaast-en-Auge, Saint Wandrille-Rançon, and Saint Xandre. Then, as a coda, they would take a huge leap to Saint Zacharie in Provence. I apologized for the distance of this final leg; I also pointed out that while a variety of saintly towns abounded in every part of France, the last two I'd indicated were the only ones in the entire country that began with x and z; and obviously strict fidelity to the alphabet should at all costs be preserved, since it had allowed me to satisfy their request so thoroughly.

Somewhat to my surprise, the couple accepted my plan without a quibble; perhaps they had intuitively sensed what was going to happen; because the plan was a success, but not in the way we expected. I received a letter from them less than two weeks after they set out. At Saint Agrève, their first stop, they had spent a few days exploring nearby back roads; and one of these had led them to a village called Rochepaule. They fell in love with the place. They found a suitable house and were now making arrangements to buy it. They had decided to travel no further than that remote valley of the Ardèche and to settle there for the rest of their days. They were sending me a case of Cornas ("it's *almost* local wine!") in gratitude for my contribution to their happiness.

Jo phoned on Bastille Day to say the shawl would be finished in a week, and please not to forget our reservation at Maxim's.

Monday, July 16, I went to see *Swan Lake* performed in the courtyard of the Louvre. It had rained violently all afternoon, but the sky cleared by evening. The temperature also dropped twenty-five degrees. The Opéra corps de ballet trailed foggy breaths that made them look like ice skaters. The cold didn't faze Nureyev or Natalia Makarova, skinny as she was. Makarova was so inspiring in the "white" tableau we even warmed ourselves up with our hectic applause. She wasn't any less thrilling in the Black Swan section. In the pas de deux she performed a series of dazzling, birdlike pirouettes before falling backwards into Nureyev's arms – and she did it again, and again; and that third time, Nureyev wasn't there. Makarova came down hard on her backside. Then she stretched out flat in what looked like terminal catalepsis. After a minute or two she was on her feet, she took up the variation where she'd left off, and she ended by leaping offstage in an ethereal jeté.

But the damage had been done; for me at least. Since the age of ten I had made a habit of escaping from the world of everyday disappointment into the paradise of art, where satisfied desire was the rule. First music, movies, poetry; later theater, painting, dance. Perfection wasn't only possible there, it was routinely achieved; or I could pretend it was, at least most of the time. Makarova's pratfall was so pitiful, so demeaning (for all of us, not only her), I felt a dream I'd been dreaming all my life had definitively ended.

I think I reacted so strongly because something else had slowly but surely been getting me down. I'd never been to Chile. If it hadn't been for my Chilean friends I probably wouldn't have cared so much about what was happening there. But through them I'd come to think of it as a happy place. And now? It too was falling on its ass. Enrique and Silvia, Isabellita and Pepe, all peaceable democrats – were they screaming at each other in the streets of Santiago? Or worse: the demos were getting violent. I winced at the thought. I was worried for them and ashamed of myself (again). It was clear who was funding the striking miners and transport workers who were paralyzing the country. Of course I wasn't personally responsible. Some consolation.

I WAS CHEERED UP BY A PHONE CALL FROM JO. SHE WAS BRINGING the finished shawl to work that afternoon. Should she drop it off at my place later? Did I want to pick it up? I said I'd pick it up, but not at the shop. I suggested the Bar Romain on Rue Caumartin after she got off work. It meant a short walk for her and a quick metro ride for me.

I almost didn't recognize her when she walked into the bar. She'd let out her thick brown hair; there was a shadow of kohl along her eyelashes and a brush of coral-tinted lipstick on her plump mouth; I wondered if she'd herself tailored the Pucci-style dress that assured her fulness so neatly. She noticed my look. "I wasn't going to show up here in my working clothes."

No one else was around. After serving our whisky sours, even the bartender disappeared. Jo had come in carrying a big plastic bag, with the shawl inside it tied up in wrapping paper. I asked her to set it between our stools. I told her we had a reservation at Maxim's at 8 P.M. the following Friday, July 27. She said she'd meet me there.

I took the metro an extra stop to Sèvres-Babylone, then walked home along Rue de Babylone, Rue Vaneau, and my own Rue de Varenne – all of them streets where it was easy to spot a tail. I closed my office curtains before opening the package and spreading its contents on the desk, under the bright light of my architect's lamp.

The shawl was five-and-a-half feet by three, a flatweave of fine wool that had been folded into the size of a large book. My designs were all there. It took me a moment to find the crucial blue and red lines because they'd been reduced to single silk threads that almost disappeared in the yarn – exactly, I thought, what Plishkin would have wanted.

The shawl was beautiful. Jo knew what colors the Khadis used, and they gave my patterns a richness I'd never imagined. I didn't look forward to selling this lovely thing.

Now I had Jo herself to look forward to. I was sure she liked me: she'd taken care to look pretty, she'd sat next to me as close as barstools allowed. I certainly liked her: she was voluptuous and exotic and bright. I also had seven months of continence behind me; total continence since my first visit to Marie-Claude Quintelpreaux – I'd been so impressed by her ritual of retention I'd even given up masturbating. I hadn't known she'd keep me waiting so long, but it seemed a shame to blow all the intensity I'd been saving up for a moment of routine relief.

She liked me all right. We'd barely settled onto the red-velvet banquette when she discreetly made this clear. But not tonight. Her husband was waiting up for her. Then when could I ever see her? I asked. She asked, Sunday afternoon? Yes, she could come to my apartment. *Voilà*, she had a more amusing plan: what about the Shapazian storeroom? She had the key. Sunday no one would bother us. It would be fun to liven up her workplace, and of course I could go on studying those wonderful rugs . . . We could always go to my apartment *afterwards*. I kissed her mouth. It was as tantalizing as it looked.

She'd cleverly taken care of the question straightaway, and I was able to enjoy the meal and her company without a qualm. We ate simply. I'd learned from Maxim's veterans that the fancy dishes on the menu were for rubes; habitués ordered things like a lamb chop or *sole meunière* – what the kitchen was really good at. We took the advice, except for dessert – Jo had *two* desserts: *profiterolles au chocolat blanc* and *crêpes flambées*. (I sucked tamely on a *sorbet au cassis.*) Wines: Meursault '66, Château Canon '59, non-vintage Krug.

Sunday I paid all my bills and answered every letter on my desk. I shined all my shoes. Finally it was time, and at 6:30 I was at the side door of the Shapazian Gallery. Jo let me in: a fleeting kiss, then she led me back to the storeroom.

Musky smell; faint light from outdoors. She'd spread out thick bright gabehs for us towards the back . "A suzani would have been sweet, but they're so fragile." We lay down. Marie-Claude Quintelpreaux had taught me that it can never last too long. To judge by her fluty gasps, Jo seemed to agree. When I began entering her, she cried out louder – she almost whinnied. I thought it was from pleasure, but she pushed me out of her: "Somebody's opened the front door. Don't say anything." How could she have heard? But now I did: men talking.

"Lie down here." She dumped my clothes after me and expertly rolled a gabeh around me into a long cylinder. "I'll tape it shut. My darling, don't budge a hair." I was rolled into a second gabeh.

I heard the metal gate being unlocked, then the older Shapazian speaking. There was muffled activity nearby – rugs being moved? In turn I was soon lifted off the floor. "*Merde*, nothing weighs that much." Shapazian: "That's one big bundle of wool, what do you expect?"

I'd been settled on a dolly. It trundled over courtyard stones, wooden floor, sidewalk (daylight at the end of my tube; a car passing). I was again lifted up and set down. Rugs landed on top of me. A car door slammed, a motor started, and I wondered how I'd keep breathing; but the drive lasted less than ten minutes. Back onto the dolly – pavement, stone floor, and a new sensation:

elevator. I was deposited on an upper floor. The castors hummed their way out of earshot.

I waited. All still. I'd rolled out of the outer gabeh when I heard men's voices approaching – other men's. They stopped a few feet away, harsh sounding.

"We are agreed? Plishkin with us. To every who listen."

"An old news."

"Resident repeats: strong smoke."

"And of instructeur other turn? Or: an dangle?"

"No. To hold black bag. Then, *Torpedo los!*"

"An torpedo? Woodsh?"

"Brno."

"Brno is gnash? *Olümle öç alinmaz.*"

"I have misunderstanding. How way out this stink place?"

Silence; same voices further off; gone. I curled an arm through the rug and ripped off one piece of tape, enough for me to wiggle out. I was in a library: three walls of twelve-foot-high dark-wood shelves; at one end a long rosewood table with Empire chairs in attendance; two Voltaire armchairs at the other. I got dressed. Past the double-leaved door there was an empty central space, with the elevator on the left and a palatial stairway opposite. I could hear social sounds upstairs, so I started down. No luck. A servitor amiably stopped me and said I'd gone one floor too far. He took me back up to a little guest washroom. That was OK with me – I needed tidying up, and I took my time doing it, hoping the valet would be gone when I came out. But there he was. He led me half-way to the next floor before stopping and gesturing me on: "And here is Monsieur himself, no doubt worried by your absence."

I was climbing towards a landing lit by gilt wall lamps and a multiplex chandelier. There were three sober Fantin-Latour portraits hanging on the walls. I looked up at an ox of a man in cream-coloured silk shirtsleeves, massive arms akimbo. He was considering me with less than curiosity.

"I'm Zendol," he announced. "You're late. Weren't you told we sit down to dinner early? Who are you?" I told him. "Don't know the name. What do you do?"

"I write."

"And what do you write?"

"Novels. Poems. I'm also a travel – "

"*You're* a poet? Well, come in, poet, and join the party."

I followed him into a dining-room, not the main one I was sure in that grand *hôtel particulier.* I think it was decorated in Wedgwood white-and-blue – it was hard to see: the only lights were ceiling spots that flooded the table like a stage. Besides which two of the five people sitting there were so unusual I couldn't take my eyes off them: a young man and woman who looked like twins (which they were), with tiny Eurasian features. They were beautiful – beautiful as Faiyoum portraits, a beauty I wanted to stare not just at but through; the beauty of a youth that would pass straight into death without ever growing old.

Zendol said to them, "Here is the 'poet' Mathews." To me: "This is Florence" (the twin), "and Jean-Baptiste" (a middle-aged gent who nodded cautiously), "Nicole" (a bored-looking, sharp-eyed, hooknosed *Parisienne*), "Harald" (the other twin, at the far end of the table), "Consuelo" (a pleasant-looking brunette – she smiled and held out her hand). "Sit next to her," which meant on his left.

Florence looked straight into my eyes when I took my seat. I looked back into hers.

Zendol: "Who brought this gentleman?"

A minute before I would have paid good money to get thrown out. Florence's black eyes changed that. She came to my rescue: "I told you Harald was bringing him." Harald sniffled.

Jean-Baptiste and Nicole returned to a discussion I'd interrupted – something about finding a name for a group, a club it sounded like. I concentrated on the food, which was passable, the wine, mediocre but welcome anyway, and the little face across the table. Eventually Consuelo was polite enough to have a private conversation with me. I asked about Harald and Florence. They fascinated her, too, but all she knew was that they were Francis Bacon's favorite models. He even paid them a retainer. "Not that he ever paints them, but he wants to make sure no one else does. He thinks they're witches." I knew what he meant.

Coffee was to be served in another room. We got up; across from me Florence dropped out of sight. I thought she'd fallen, hurried over to help her, and almost knocked her down as she came round the table.

She was forty inches tall – a true midget, perfect in every limb. I wanted to lift her into my arms. She took my hand. "We must get to know each other."

The coffee room was disappointing – contemporary French furniture, a couple of recent Buffets, geometrical rugs. After the coffee Zendol served pear brandy from Brittany. He said an old friend made it; it tasted as though he'd washed his feet in it.

Zendol started needling me. He couldn't believe anyone tall and athletic-looking could be a poet. I said I'd published novels, too, one right here in France with Gallimard. Yes, but any thug could write novels – what about the poetry? Only one small collection, I admitted (not mentioning it had been mimeographed by a non-commercial enthusiast in Leeds); but my poems had appeared in lots of literary magazines – my "perverbial poems" were in the latest issue of *Poetry Review*. I was asked to explain the meaning of "perverbial poem," this led to my talking about the Oulipo, and a couple of the guests by now were getting interested and started telling our host to leave me alone. I was even invited to recite one of my French *poèmes à perverbes*.

"*Très joli*," Consuelo pronounced, I smiled, and Zendol popped his cork. "If this guy's a poet, he can prove it. He can make up a poem right now. Of course we'll help him out – we'll give him some lovely words to rhyme with. Two from each of us." He paused. "Here are my two – forgive me, Mathews, my English is limited: *swastika* and *haddock*." He was visibly gloating.

Florence refused to go along. Nicole thought the game was amusing and proposed *jonquil* and *plectrum*. That was fair enough: hard rhymes are a traditional part of *bouts rimés*. Jean-Baptiste hesitated before deciding on *gardenia* and *farthing*. Harald blew his nose.

"Never mind, that's plenty," Zendol said. "Now," he asked me, "are you familiar with the Squat?"

"Sure!" I smiled some more. I *loved* the Squat. It had been the rage the past few months, and I'd danced it whenever I could. Upbeat music; funny, sexy steps. Hard work, too, since you had to perform an actual squat every time the word was sung. I took off my jacket and tie.

"So I will play a sample Squat and you will invent new words to it, *n'est-ce pas ?*"

I had nothing to lose. Zendol's dare gave me a chance to shut him up, as well as show off to Florence. I danced pretty well, my voice wasn't bad, and as for the improv, I'd played rhyming games before.

Zendol put on an LP. The tune he chose turned out to be "Watergate Squat" from Air America's last album. I took my time clearing away the rugs. When I'd finished, I had the tune down pat. "Can we start over?"

I danced through the opening instrumental introduction and started singing as soon as the vocal began:

Not bitch fascist (squat!) with swastika
And bumper (squat!) double-cross sticker
Let's anagram (squat!) and acrostic her
Let's lock her in a paddock
In six feet of rotten haddock
Sing high (squat!), speak low (squat!)
Ho heigh (squat!), heigh ho (squat!)
Then we'll go play chess (squat!) life-size in Marostica!
Squat squat squat,
Squat squat

But girl as fair (squat!) as spring jonquil
Turns me on (squat!) more than plonk will
Without her I'll (squat!) never be tronquil
I drink to her in select rum
Pluck her sweet chords with my plectrum
Sing high (squat!), speak low (squat!)
Ho heigh (squat!), heigh ho (squat!)
I'll write her fine praises (squat!) with my feathery long quill
Squat squat squat,
Squat squat

The squatting was taking the breath out of me. Every time I turned, my head sprayed sweat. But Florence was watching me with the sweetest smile.

Maybe seen from far (squat!) or maybe seen near
So sweetly (squat!) sweetly teeny her
Face as disputed (squat!) as Ruthenia
No other's worth a farthing
Not in painting or in carving
Sing high (squat!), speak low (squat!)
Ho heigh (squat!), heigh ho (squat!)
For her I'll hide my heart (squat!), my heart in this
gardenia.
Squat squat squat,
Squat squat
In this gardenia
Squat squat squat,
Squat squat
In this gardenia
Squat squat squat squat squat squat squat squat

Squat.

When Jean-Baptiste had first said gardenia, I'd taken my breast-pocket handkerchief and folded it to look, sort of, like a white flower. I'd left it on a table near the sofa where Florence was sitting. On my final run of squats I picked it up and on the last chord of the song knelt in front of her and offered her my "gardenia." She laughed and clapped her hands – the others were clapping too – then took my handkerchief and began wiping the sweat from my face and neck. She went on smiling as she said to me, "I thought you'd never stop. Can't you see what they're doing? You're being set up. You've been picked to play patsy."

"Patsy?"

"I've got to get you out of here. It's a good thing I like you."

Consuelo was bending over me: "'Marostica' – *absolument*

génial!" Marostica: where human chessmen act out a game on the checkered town square. Zendol had gone, the fink.

Florence: "Now get up and follow me." She turned to the others: "He needs a towel."

We were barely out of the room when she started running towards the back of the house. Down one corridor and another. "I know it's dark. This is the way." She stopped at a door that opened onto a faintly lighted, narrow circular staircase. We hurried down.

"What's going on?"

"Darling, how could you be so dumb? Don't you know these people?"

"I never laid eyes on them."

"You never heard of Zendol? Ordre Nouveau?"

Down two floors; two to go. "Ordre Nouveau, yes, the right-wing – "

"Fascists. All of them. Except Harald and me. The *SDEC* is coming for them tonight, with cops. They found out and decided to pin whatever they've done on you." The S.D.E.C.E. was the principal French intelligence service, the *Service de documentation étrangère et de contre-espionnage*, in conversation always referred to as *le SDEC* (pronounced *zdek*).

"Florence, I was brought here by mistake."

"So they improvised. But that's why Zendol made sure you stayed. You'll be all right now."

On the ground floor Florence unlocked a narrow door that led out of the house. Not out of doors, though: we walked into a cool interior, dark and vast, with no lights except for a few candles burning here and there. There was a residual smell of incense. Florence pulled me across the empty church towards the altar, where the candles were brightest. In front of it she stopped and turned: "Kiss me!" Minnow tongue. "Now take me. Quickly. I have to get back, and don't worry about my being small. It will be good for me. I promise."

The altar was covered with a sheet and a sort of velvet rug. I picked her up and laid her over it. I moved the candles closer – she'd opened and folded back her blouse and skirt, she wasn't wearing anything else, the mauve silk wreathing the glow of her nakedness was almost black in that soft light. I bent over to kiss her. She pulled me towards her. She loosened my own clothing and took my confused member between her delicate feet: their cool sheath coaxing me slyly. I responded, all would soon have been well if another light hadn't started moving in the back of the church, half hidden by the choir screen.

"Someone's here."

"Merde!" She sat up and looked round. "It's the sexton. You'll be all right. *Adieu!*"

She picked up her things and went trotting off barefoot into the darkness. I heard the little door pull shut. I buttoned myself up and prostrated myself full-length in front of the crucifix.

"What a surprise!" – words spoken melodiously. "Might this be a straggler from vespers?"

I got onto my knees, eyes closed, lips moving silently. I crossed myself before standing up. "Forgive me. I so needed a moment of special prayer – "

"I do understand."

" – I apologize for the intrusion, moving the candles – "

"A pretty young thing like you needn't apologize."

My forty-three years were not reassured by his words. The sexton was small, gentle-looking, and horribly white. "You see, I came here because of a vow, a vow of chastity – "

To my relief he smiled and nodded understandingly. "I see. Well, I am under a vow myself. It is of a different kind. I took it many years ago, and I intend to keep it forever – not your case, I trust." He gave me a kindly appraising look before continuing:

"I was vacationing in Corsica with my beloved companion. His name was Mamadu. We had rented a Sharki in Ajaccio – a ketch about twelve meters long, a most reliable boat. We headed south, leaving the Îles Sanguinaires far behind us, passing Cap di Muro before we moored for the night in Propriano, at the head of the Golfe de Valinco. Next morning we rounded Cap Senetosa and followed that long wild coast until we reached the Bouches de Bonifacio.

"There was a mild following wind and we were sailing wing-and-wing. The Corsican coast was still to port; way to the south Sardinia emerged; and the expanse of the Tyrrhenian opened before us. Mamadu, who had been plucking his *kora* and enchanting the airs with song, now moved up to the bow to view the prospect, sitting on the pulpit with his back against the forestay; or so I supposed, since he was hidden from my sight by the mainsail on one side and the genoa on the other. Every so often he would shout out a delighted word or two. Then there came a spell when I heard nothing. I called his name several times. There was no answer, so I pushed the tiller to starboard, bringing the boat to a broad reach so that I could see the bow. No one was there. There was no sign of him in the water. I came about, it seemed to take a lifetime to get the boat turned into the wind. For three hours I tacked back and forth over the same stretch of sea. Nothing, nothing.

"He was beautiful. His skin was luminous, a black so deep it looked blue, like Siberian anthracite. When I came back to Paris, I made my vow: in his memory I would become as white as he was black. I haven't gone out in daylight since. Only at night. Otherwise I stay here" – he smiled faintly – "minding my keys and pews. Please take my card. If ever . . ."

He let me out through the priest's door. I was in Auteuil, on a little street off Avenue Mozart. I'd been in the church of Les Six Saints Jean, famous for its frequentation by the Napoleonic nobility. Many of its members were buried there, and one of them had probably built the house where Zendol lived. I found a taxi and went home.

I PHONED PATRICK THE NEXT DAY, BUT HE'D LEFT TOWN FOR the week.

At least he was coming back soon. Most people weren't. Paris's August exodus was under way; many of my acquaintances had gone away already to avoid the crush. There wouldn't be another Oulipo meeting till August 31. Restaurants closed, including Le Balzar. So did my gym (the Institut Guénot, on Boulevard Saint-Germain, where I worked out three times a week). There was no place in my neighborhood where you could buy a baguette or a head of lettuce.

Marie-Claude Quintelpreaux finally answered a note that had been forwarded to her in Tuscany: she wouldn't be back before mid September.

Not a word from Jo, although I had some news about her from the younger Shapazian. He arrived unannounced at my apartment late Tuesday morning. He'd heard I'd come into possession of a "rare weaving" from Central Asia.

"You mean my Mesopotamian kilim? It's hanging over there by the bed."

"I do not mean a kilim, or a gabeh, or a magic carpet. I mean a map."

"What makes you think I have a map?"

"It's my business to know."

I'd alerted some clients to the arrival of my "document;" I didn't remember being so specific about it. Not even Jo knew it was a map. "That's strange. Tell me, are you still getting rugs in from Iran and Afghanistan?"

"Yes, excellent ones. They're selling very well."

"Is that nice woman still working in the back room? Arikia, a name like that?"

"She is no longer with us. Please stop putting me off and show me what I came to see." His voice was hard. I brought out the shawl. Standing by the window, Shapazian opened it fold by fold and turned it slowly in the light. He paid no attention to my account of its Khadistanian provenance.

"Good weave; a little slack." After a pause: "So blue gives the basis." (That was true: blue thread outlined the purely geographical features. It was what is called a false-color map.) "I'm glad to see the Tura is returning at last to its original bed. I don't care how he got it out. I'll take it."

I explained that I had several prospective buyers.

"No doubt. But this is my line of work, and I get to do the selling." He took out a bundle of fresh bills and counted off five thousand dollars. "You wouldn't get half that from any of them." He was in no mood for argument.

I spent two days anxiously explaining to my clients that I'd been forced to let the "document" go before I could show it to them. They weren't surprised. The milieu was highly competitive and things like that were bound to happen. They all asked me to describe the item, and since it was out of my hands, I saw no reason not to.

When I met Patrick on Friday, I told him about my Sunday adventures and asked for his interpretation of them. He couldn't be absolutely sure, of course, but it sounded to him as if they were due to pure chance. Nobody besides Jo knew I was inside those rugs. Zendol and his friends had either mistaken me for someone else, or they'd treated my unforeseen appearance as a windfall to exploit, just as Florence had suggested. Patrick confirmed her description of Zendol. He was a notorious right-wing activist and had already been taken to court for inciting violence.

He didn't think I'd been compromised in any way, but why didn't I go someplace else for a while to be on the safe side? After I'd escaped last Sunday, Zendol might have given my name to the authorities in the hope of setting me up later on. Not likely, but possible. When I told him about Shapazian's visit, he said in mock horror, "My God, leave town before someone else gets interested in you!"

SOMEONE ELSE *DID* GET INTERESTED IN ME, NO LATER THAN THE following morning. An American named Bud Mirdan called and said he would like to meet me. Since he'd heard about me through Groff, I assumed he was a prospective business client. I agreed to have a drink with him at the bar of the Crillon late that afternoon.

He was waiting for me at a corner table when I arrived. Mirdan was a short, slender man in his fifties, with thick matted gray hair, a long, sad face, and tiny hands. I accepted the dry martini he recommended. After some inevitable small talk, I asked why he wanted to see me.

He explained that he and his colleagues were in a line of work similar to my own. "I don't mean the travel side, that's irrelevant. We're like you in that we do research and consulting for a number of organizations, including the U.S. Government. We've been wondering if you'd be interested in collaborating with us in some way that would benefit us all. The point would be sharing information with each other. That's what's really impressed us about you – you've been working on your own as far as we can tell, and in a short time you've managed to contact a bunch of damned interesting people. That's a talent we can use."

His tone was quiet, friendly, and reasonable – I was intrigued; I was almost tempted. He went on:

"The relationship can be set up almost any way you like. We can buy your company and give you a salary to go on running it – there'd be no interference on our part beyond having privileged access to whatever you find out. Or we can hire you on a case-by-case basis whenever there are assignments that could benefit from your particular qualifications. Or we can pay you for information as it shows up. You'll be paid, whatever the deal, and paid well."

"You have to understand I'm only the secretary of the business. Obviously I'll have to consult Madame Sosnowska."

Mirdan was speechless; not for long. He smiled his winning, crinkly smile: "Somehow I don't think she'll care one way or the other."

It was an exciting offer. It meant moving up to the big leagues. That was the problem. Mirdan's confident manner had convinced me he was a pro. (Except perhaps for the Soviet Tourist Department, no one else had questioned Elzbieta Sosnowska's existence.) It wouldn't take him and his colleagues much time to see through my amateurish ways; even if they didn't, I'd soon lose control of what I did or didn't do. I'd be in way over my head.

"I have to say no. There's too much at stake for me to risk working long-term with anybody else. I can't go into it. It's a personal problem. I wish I could tell you how much I appreciate your getting in touch with me. In normal circumstances I wouldn't hesitate, not for a second."

"Here's a bonbon or two more for you to consider. Part of the agreement is that we'll pass on *all* information relevant to your travel business. Then it seems to me that your communications equipment is (to put it politely) rather basic. We can upgrade that for you immediately. We can even supply you with a radio transmitter that will connect you directly to our correspondents around the world. At any time of day you could find out in two minutes if those midnight buses in Bolivia are running on schedule."

I laughed, then shook my head. "I'm sorry. It's just not possible."

"Fair enough. Why don't you think it over? Call this number if you change your mind." He handed me a slip of paper. "My secretary will answer. Her name's Josie Soccor. She'll know who you are."

I would find out only later what this meeting signified.

I no longer had any reason to stay in Paris. I didn't leave right away because Georges Perec reappeared unexpectedly. He insisted that I come with him to a rehearsal of a play that Richard Foreman was preparing for the fall. What I saw turned me into a lifelong Foreman devotee; but I soon realized that something else had contributed to Georges's enthusiasm: Kate Manheim, Richard's companion, was a strikingly beautiful, sexy woman, and she couldn't resist casting her spell on practically every man she met. Georges claimed to be passionately in love with her and announced that after his movie was finished he was moving to New York to live with her. I made no comment. I hoped he wouldn't be let down too hard.

During those last days in the city I noticed two news items. The first was Natalia Makarova's announcement that she would no longer have Nureyev as a partner. The second was a report that soon after it crashed, the remains of the Tupolev-144 had been carried off by American agents.

Where should I go? Follow Marie-Claude Quintelpreaux to her Tuscan village? I couldn't imagine that she was there all by herself. Look for Marie Chaix in Provence? I was still haunted by her, but her husband might object to my haunting her. Anyway, Tuscany and Provence were unbearably hot at that time of year. So I headed for my own house in the Vercors. Loulou, the man who looked after it when I was away, met me at the Grenoble station on August 10 and drove me home. As always, the mere sight of the place made me happy. However, my long absence had meant that a real nuisance would be waiting for me: weeds.

I had no real garden; there were only irregular planted areas around the house. What grew in them was the result of luck, the ability to survive, and spasmodic initiatives on my part. The conditions for gardening were difficult – a mountain climate, limy soil, shade or half-shade almost everywhere – so if a plant took, I tended to let it be. It wasn't a rational approach, and a green disorder was the most I could hope for. Furthermore, unless I was able to clear things out by the end of June, weeding was a nightmare: the growing season was short and weeds spread fast. That August afternoon I saw that I had hours of work ahead – everything from easily yanking up three-inch seedling firs and ashtrees to prying dandelions and plantains out of crevices; from chasing gooseweed through layers of periwinkles to extracting the devious root-systems of vetch from underneath columbines and foxgloves.

In general the house was full of things waiting to be done. There were hundreds of books on the shelves that I'd never read. The Pleyel baby grand, recently tuned, kept reminding me how much my fingers were out of practice. I'd stacked great beech trunks at the back of the yard: they needed sawing up and splitting. A radiator leaked. Fuses had to be replaced.

None of this was upsetting, and certainly not the way it would have been a couple of years before, when I was neurotically obsessed by housekeeping. (I sometimes actually screamed out loud if I found spoons put back in the wrong drawer.) Since then, eleven years after his mother left, my son had run away. My family haven was turned into a family mausoleum. I decided to sell it. And I did sell it, to some nondescript Englishman. My real-estate agent in Grenoble negotiated with his *notaire* in Paris for several weeks – long enough for me to say goodbye to my neighbors, who were the salt of the earth, and get used to giving up a place I'd worked and dreamed in for thirteen years. I went up to Paris with my agent's assistant to sign the contract. The Englishman backed off – the *notaire* said the water supply wasn't reliable. I was surprised, I was angry, and before long I realized how lucky I was. I was now the owner of an attractive place that had been stripped of its psychological garbage. I didn't give a hoot where anyone put my spoons.

So this August I started spending my time doing what I'd always done: gardening, repairing, hiking, practicing the piano, reading, cooking myself good meals, collecting wildflowers. I worked hard at these things, and they kept me very busy. I did some writing, not much – poems, a short short story, Oulipian doodles – enough to feel I could still call myself a writer, enough to ward off any gloomy demons that might still be lurking in the surrounding depths of fir and spruce.

During my second week in Lans, Andrée phoned to suggest we go for a hike that afternoon. A nice idea – it would be good to forget my domestic preoccupations, good to see her again, even if our romantic involvement was long over. If she mentioned CIA matters, I was ready to give her an earful.

She drove us up the valley of the Furon, to the east of my house, till we came to the end of the paved road. We planned to climb to the top of the Moucherotte, 6000 feet high, with a view of Grenoble and the massifs around it – Belledonne, les Écrins, la Grande Chartreuse. An easy three-hour climb, with late-flowering plants all along the way – yarrow, sheep's bit, buttercups, fireweed; then Canterbury bells and small scabious where deciduous trees took over (with bright-berried rowan among them); higher still, among evergreens that again predominated, eyebright and big yellow gentians; and finally meadows that had just started to yellow and were full of blue-gray pinks, with no trees at all except a few hunched pines.

It was there that a flock of tiny piping dark-brown birds flitted past and settled near us in the grass. They made Andrée laugh with pleasure; I asked what they were. "The people here call them *petits pieds*."

Petits pieds: little feet. The two words made me sick with lust: Florence rolling my erection between her cool soles . . . I turned to Andrée, took her in my arms, and tried to kiss her. She hissed, "Are you crazy?," pushing me away as she looked around her. No one in sight, but we were visible for miles.

Later: "What came over you? If you want to get back together – I don't know. But remember, we're not sixteen any more."

Patrick called on September 1 to say he was in Grenoble and could he visit – perhaps tomorrow, since it was Sunday? We'd spend the day together, and he'd go back down to town for his dinner engagement. I was all for it.

It was warm, sunny weather. We ate lunch under a parasol in the courtyard. Cold *faux filet*, romaine-and-tomato salad, two local cheeses (Saint Marcellin, which is a cow cheese made like goat cheese, and Sassenage, an almost sweet blue); with a bottle and a half of Cornas, the mild sort that can be drunk young.

At one point Patrick returned to the subject of Zendol. He'd looked up someone he knew who was friendly with him and asked him if he couldn't find out what had really happened that Sunday night. His friend obliged. According to his own account, Zendol hadn't any idea who I was or how I happened to be there, and he hadn't cared – all kinds of people showed up at his house. As for making me the fall guy for some trouble he was in, that was hokum. Florence had made the story up as a way of having me to herself. She couldn't resist a new man, and she never wasted time going after him. I'd been a great success with the other guests.

After lunch I showed Patrick the house. He insisted on seeing every inch, even the attic, which was littered with old skis and skipoles, snowshoes, tennis rackets, suitcases, toys, empty wine bottles, and dormouse droppings. I drove him past Villard-de-Lans to Corrençon, an unspoiled village ten miles south, to let him see how wild and vast the massif really was. Melancholy end-of-summer light was over everything.

"For an intelligence officer, you've got the fall-back place of your dreams."

"Hiding here's not that easy. Not in wintertime, for sure."

"It's a place to disappear from. A dozen high trails to choose from, then over the mountains and out the other side."

Back at the house Patrick and I had a parting glass of Clairette de Die. I never saw him again.

That night I heard the first dormice of the season scurrying overhead. (Sometimes they played loud soccer games with walnuts stolen from a basket in the living-room.) They were getting ready for their winter sleep. Dormice are clever, fast, and pretty, but I did my best to keep their numbers down – my house was their favorite in the village, and they flocked to it. So I live-trapped as many as I could and released them in the forest, farther away than any dormouse was supposed to travel. Fat chance.

I WENT BACK TO PARIS ON SEPTEMBER 10. ON THE TRAIN I READ through the *Herald Tribune* – I'd hardly seen a paper in a month. There were several articles about Chile. While the country fell apart, joint naval maneuvers with the U.S. were being held as scheduled. According to one dispatch, Chilean authorities had refused entrance to a navy band all of whose members were, amazingly, commissioned officers: Lieutenant Commander Stephen Fassbender (clarinet), Lieutenant (jg) Arthur Kominsky (bass drum), Lieutenant Harold J. Duboise (euphonium), and so on – a grotesque ruse to get intelligence officers into Santiago. I wanted to laugh, but the news spelled trouble coming.

I told my taxi to drop me at my corner café, Le Varenne. I was having an espresso at the counter when I saw at a sidewalk table the knobby head of Eugenius Schmidt, the man who'd first mentioned Plishkin to me. Could he be there on my account? Why not? "Monsieur Schmidt!" He was wearing the same black suit and white nylon shirt. He latched onto me like a terrier.

"H. Mathews! Lastly! Dear H. Mathews! I earnestly awaiting opportunity to resee you. And you are here!" He grabbed my bag. "Let me to carry with you into your home, necessary you are tire ending journey. Not I think from Sverdlovsk! I use many times subjecting mentalwise to trans-Siberian traveling plans. I necessary tell you Plishkin no more arrest to house, he is integrational absolute with ulterior organs." By now he'd forced his way after me into my apartment. "Little charming flat! Is your fuck-place?" He examined my office, wondered where my transmitter was, and started looking for it in the bedroom-living-room. Turning back the kilim hanging by my bed, he exclaimed, “Oh, oh! H. Mathews! Mirror! I guess not say to Marie-Claude. What? My friend Mademoiselle Quintelpreaux lead me to lecture offering Soviet travel. Never telling you? However she say of you lot, she affect you great.” He turned on the light in the kitchen (“Just usual shit”), investigated the entrance closet where I grew marijuana by artificial light, then pushed me back into the office. “You have strange talent Marie-Claude observe, hard in defining, I call ‘meditation negative.’ You volunteer imaging evils, you be staying calm. Please do this to me. How? You write! Schmidt needing mantras, also maybe koans, parodoxisms. H. Mathews, I am pregnancy of bad ghosts, you help me discharge such ghosts. Sitting before table, write, go, *go*! Think only: Schmidt misfits, lust, lie, murder, betray, you say it. Write short, out of top of hat. Like ‘Squat, squat.’ Yes. ‘Thumb in nose, blood flows.’ OK. More! More again! I read after, I trust. You trust not, not importance. Two more, promise, Schmidt gone. Is cellar with flat? Sure, other time.”

He was no sooner out the door than I was on the phone to Patrick for advice about this nosy comedian. No answer; none at his office number next morning.

Later at Le Varenne the owner handed me a message. It was from the Frenchman who’d sent me to Graz. On Saturday I was scheduled to pick up another package in Saint Sulpice. He was counting on me.

Leaving that kind of note in a café seemed risky. I certainly didn’t want people in the neighborhood to think I was mixed up in any funny business.

I READ IN THE MORNING'S *TRIB* THAT MEMBERS OF THE CHILEAN and American navies had been caught putting up a radio transmitter on an isolated promontory north of Valparaiso. Allende had refused Admiral Montero's resignation, but Montero was the last of the three commanders who had pledged fidelity to democratic process, and how long could he hang on? Two days before, air force units had fought a battle against armed workers south of the capital. Doctors, medical personnel, professional employees, shopkeepers, bus drivers, all had joined the trucker's strike. Inflation was running at 343%.

None of this news was on the front page. The putsch that day surprised a lot of people. I could hardly believe it myself. I should have remembered Guatemala; but I hadn't had friends there. By mid afternoon Allende was dead. The U.S. Navy, which must have provided the rebels with radio communication up and down the coast, went steaming innocently away into the Atlantic.

I was smothered in shame, in "patriotic shame." Personal shame, too. This was more than my old frailty in the face of public events. With or without evidence, every thinking person would assume CIA had been involved. That meant me.

I read the news Wednesday morning. I unplugged my phone. I stayed home for three days, only going out to buy food and the morning and evening newspapers. I kept hoping the situation would change, knowing it wouldn't. The U.S. were going to recognize the new Chilean government. Its active support of the putsch was generally acknowledged. I'd made myself party to a monstrosity.

My game had to end. I'd go back to being the fool who kept denying what he was supposed to be. Better to be taken for a fool than an accomplice. I'd been a fool anyway thinking I could play spy and not pay for it.

Saturday I reconnected the phone. I called Loulou and told him to go to my house and turn off the answering machine.

The first incoming call was from Georges Perec. He was spending September editing *Un Homme qui dort* in a suburb of Tunis; but he'd flown back to Paris for a few days to see his analyst. This brought a little light into my soul. Georges was the only friend I could confide in. He'd probably think I was a fool, too, but he'd do his best by me.

Georges had an ongoing project called "a tentatively exhaustive study of several Parisian localities." Once a season he'd go back to each of these places for a few hours and write down whatever he saw there. One venue was Place Saint Sulpice; he was going there that same afternoon; and thanks to my mysterious assignment, so was I. After retrieving the designated package from the church, I met Georges at the Café de la Mairie. On the table in front of him there was a bottle of Perrier, a notebook, and his big Mont Blanc pen. He was setting down the pen when I joined him.

"That's the fifth time the woman with an empty stroller has gone by."

"So what does that mean?"

"It means a woman with an empty stroller has gone by five times."

He was looking at me. "Something wrong?"

I nodded. "I have to drop this off at the Fac de Droit. Can you come along?"

It wasn't far to Rue d'Assas – two blocks down Rue Madame, two more across Rue de Fleurus. I had time to tell him about my great Idea. "So that's what you've been up to!" He sounded amused. "Is it fun?"

A burly man whose hat had a tassel in the place of the usual ribbon was standing on the law school steps. I went up to him and gave him the parole: "*Il paraît qu'il va pleuvoir.*" He replied, "*Ce ne sont que des racontars,*" and I handed him the package. He went into the building. Georges: "Do you know who that guy is?"

"No. Who is he?"

"A fascist shit named Roger Holeindre. You shouldn't go near people like that."

"I've never even met him. I was doing a friend a favor."

We started walking towards Luxembourg Gardens. I told Georges I'd given up my project because of Chile.

"What did you expect?"

"I didn't expect to feel responsible."

"You aren't responsible."

"I've done all I could to identify myself with people who are."

"It was naval intelligence that did the job. CIA was only marginally involved. At least that's the word from the Chilean embassy."

"But I didn't know that. And nobody else will, either."

"Tell me everything."

We sat on a park bench until I was through my story. Georges was still amused. "You didn't harm anybody. It's over now. *Basta!*"

We walked across the fifth arrondissement to Avenue des Gobelins and dinner Chez Marty. I felt better.

Marie-Claude Quintelpreaux phoned Sunday morning to arrange a visit that afternoon. I needed to see her; and talk to her, too.

She appeared in her usual blue caftan and started leading me towards the incense and muted lights. I said, "You know I'm lost once we start. You've got to explain something first or it'll spoil whatever we do." I asked her about Eugenius Schmidt.

"Oh, Eugène!" She laughed.

"That's his real name?"

"Isn't he a number? Of course I'll explain. You see, I do have a brother after all. But he's no recluse. He runs a travel agency on the Champs-Élysées. He thought you might be competition and sent me to your lecture to check you out. Eugène's his man for Central Europe, so I brought him along."

"Is he deeply insane, or is that his English?"

"He's saner in German, and in Turkish, so I hear. Come. This will be our last rehearsal . . ."

I'd been waiting for these words for months. Suddenly I was immensely happy.

We knelt facing one another, naked as usual, with our knees almost touching. We didn't move, we only leaned forward slightly so that we could stare into the other's eyes – one eye at a time, we were so close. A quarter of an hour, then another and another, that's what I calculated afterwards. At the moment there was only that one moment going on and on and on. I was embarrassed, and then bored, and distracted, and anxious, and confused. What I saw turned red or green or swirled in mixed streaky colors. None of that mattered. I went on staring. I started falling through her iris. There were animals inside her eye, snakes, faces (hello, Eugenius Schmidt), twilight woods, nightmare caverns; and then nothing. Nothing except her eye and her, or us – we coexisted in an apparently boundless continuum of emptiness. I thought, why, this is love beyond imagining. I'd quietly started crying. When Marie-Claude leaned away, she was crying a little, too. A hint of bitterness when she looked away?

"We've come far enough." She put on her caftan. I followed her into the front room, where she handed me a sealed business envelope. "It's nice having a brother in the travel business. Inside there are two roundtrip tickets to – never mind. You'll find out when you open it. And don't open it till next Friday – promise? You'll still have time to pack your things. For our consummation." There were tears in her eyes again when she kissed me goodbye.

I set off for home through Sunday gaggles of families, tourists, and students. As I was crossing Rue de Rennes, Jim West stopped me; he and Mary McCarthy lived down the street. I told him how sick I felt about Chile. He didn't comment and only shook his head dubiously. "I'm glad they're taking better care of you." I must have looked blank. "Aren't you running a travel agency now? It may not be great, but at least it's cover."

Jim worked at the embassy: he should have known better. I didn't say anything.

I SPENT TWO DAYS DISMANTLING LOCUS SOLUS. I SENT NOTES TO all concerned announcing that its offices had been closed and its services discontinued. I phoned AARO and asked to have my listing omitted from its Directory. I wrote an application to the phone company to have my Paris and Lans phone numbers changed – I requested "as soon as possible," knowing it might take a year.

Wednesday I found a note from Georges in my mailbox: "Urgent. The victor of the nearby computational street summons you to return to the same fishy troop when a first point has been scored by his racket." (*Le vainqueur d'une rue à calcul voisine vous somme de rejoindre la même troupe poissonnière dès que sa raquette marquera le premier point.*)

I took the note with me to Le Varenne for my mid-morning espresso. The owner seemed a little cool towards me. Yves Cauchy, the helpful neighboring concierge, had acted the same way three days earlier; at the time I'd thought, Sunday grumps.

I reread Georges's message. He was a professional inventor of crossword puzzles, and these phrases sounded like crossword definitions; so I set to work solving them. My first clue came with "fishy troop": that was what would ordinarily be called a school of fish. The French word for a school of fish is *banc*; and a *banc* is also a bench. If "the same fishy troop" translated as "the same bench," it must mean the one where Georges and I had sat together a few days before. Then "the nearby computational street" was Rue de Fleurus: because *calcul* means not only computation but "stone" (as in kidney-stone); and Rue de Fleurus had been home to Gertrude Stone, aka Stein. (Later my Petit Larousse taught me that the battle of Fleurus was one of Marshal de Luxembourg's greatest victories.) As for "a first point scored by his racket," in tennis the first point is called as "fifteen;" and 15 hours is 3 P.M. by the twenty-four-hour clock.

That's when I showed up at Luxembourg Gardens, wondering what the fuss was about.

"YOU'VE GOT YOURSELF INTO DEEP SHIT. AND ME WITH YOU!" The last words upset me, and it must have showed. Georges quickly added, "Oh, I'll be OK. But I told you Holeindre was bad news. You remember Laurent Duchamp?"

I'd met him one afternoon two years before in Georges's old apartment on Rue de Seine. He was a political writer, a devotee of left-wing causes. I'd only seen him in passing since.

Laurent had been visiting Chile and been expelled right after the putsch. He had an old friend from his student days who was now working in S.D.E.C.E.; his specialty was illegal right-wing activity. He and Laurent had an agreement to informally share any information that came their way; so Laurent had naturally contacted his friend to report on Pinochet and his crowd. It so happened that the previous day – Monday – the friend had seen a photograph of Roger Holeindre meeting Georges and me on Rue d'Assas.

The S.D.E.C.E. officer couldn't understand Georges's being there – he was left-wing and Jewish, and Holeindre was a militant racist. He phoned Laurent, and Laurent phoned Georges. Georges told him he'd tagged along while I did a friend a favor. The officer then told Laurent that there were other compromising reports about me. Georges swore I'd never been involved in any political activity since May '68, at least not in France.

"Laurent doesn't know what to think. He says you've got yourself mixed up with some extremist network. You'd better talk to him yourself."

I told him two minutes were all I'd need to clear myself with any reasonable listener. Georges said I was a sentimental optimist; I told him he was a sentimental pessimist.

Laurent was in great demand as an eyewitness of Allende's downfall, but Georges successfully argued him into having an early dinner with us Friday. We met at the apartment Georges was renting on Avenue de Ségur and settled for a meal of gnocchi and cold cuts; I think Laurent was leery of being seen with me in public. He certainly treated me cautiously, at first in any case. I was very jittery – I was starting to feel genuinely worried. Georges kept me calm enough to give Laurent a coherent acount of my play-acting. When I'd finished he said, "It's got to be true. Nobody'd make up an alibi as goofy as that."

He summarized what he'd learned from his friend. Ever since World War II, French counterintelligence and its counterparts in Germany and Italy had consistently infiltrated the extreme right-wing groups in their countries. For the past couple of months their informants had reported that on several occasions I'd been identified as the person responsible for the death of Christa Knemius, the left-wing activist who'd been killed by a bomb in Milan on April 12. I'd been there on that date. The type of bomb used was one often supplied by CIA – a similar one had blown up Mahmoud Hamchari in Paris last January.

"That's how *le SDEC* was tipped off. A young woman whiz from Mossad was assigned to that case. She told your people, your people told my people – "

"They're not 'my people'."

"You think I have anything to do with this shit?"

"All right. Don't 'your people' know better?"

“Of course. The problem is: there’s so-called evidence out in the world linking you to a bunch of fascist thugs, and it’s being spread through left-wing circles all over Europe. I wasn’t around or I’d probably have heard it myself.”

“But that’s crazy.”

“So? Listen, my *SDEC* friend trusts me. I’ll see what I can do. But he says it’s bad. He told me you should have left the country weeks ago.”

Who was spreading this poison, and why? It was laughable to think I could plan and effectuate a bomb-killing. Whenever I poured a drink I’d be doing well to just spill it and not break the glass. When I carved a chicken, I sometimes included the end of my thumb. If I ever set off a bomb, I’d be its first victim. Of course strangers wouldn’t know that.

Even before Laurent’s worrying confirmation of what Georges had told me, I’d decided I had to find Patrick and ask him for advice. He wasn’t answering his home phone, and I realized he still hadn’t given me his home address, although I knew he lived somewhere on Plaine Monceau. No response at his business number either; so that afternoon I’d gone to the office of Zapata Petroleum to see if they knew how to reach him. The receptionist told me that was no problem at all, he was right here in his office. She announced me by phone, led me down a corridor, and opened a door on a small, prematurely bald, bespectacled man sitting behind a paper-strewn desk. The man stood up and asked politely what he could do for me.

“I’m looking for a friend, Patrick Burton-Cheyne.”

“I didn’t know we were friends. But you’re looking at Patrick Burton-Cheyne.”

I quickly found out that Patrick’s business number had never been in use at Zapata. I asked Mr. Burton-Cheyne if by chance he'd ever written an article on John Ashbery's poetry. Yes, he had, ages ago. He hesitated before adding:

"I'm afraid meeting me hasn't been exactly pleasant for you – in fact, you look as though you'd swallowed a dozen dead oysters. If there's anything I can do – "

"No. Thank you. It hasn't anything to do with you at all. It's not something I can easily explain."

"I see. Do at least tell me one thing: how is John Ashbery these days? I haven't heard from him in years. If you're in touch with him, be sure to give him my best."

I ONLY WENT OUT SATURDAY TO BUY THE PAPERS AND HAVE A quick coffee at Le Varenne; I didn't want to miss hearing from Laurent. Georges called at 7 that evening and told me to meet him for dinner at La Sologne on Rue de Bellechasse; we weren't known there. It was a subdued meal. Georges said Laurent's *SDEC* friend had agreed to see me the following day. He was taking a big risk: I must never mention the meeting to anyone.

The arrangements were as follows. Laurent would phone me on some pretext around 1:45 P.M. I'd then go straight to Le Saint Germain at the corner of Bac and Raspail and order coffee at the counter. When a tan Simca 1100 pulled up outside the café, I'd quickly get into the seat next to the driver. "Wear jeans and your old windbreaker. Please, *no* dark glasses."

Laurent called early Sunday afternoon, and I had my ear to the receiver halfway through the first ring. He calmly asked me how he could reach someone in the Oulipo, I forget whom – I gave him the number and he hung up. At Le Saint Germain my coffee was drunk and paid for five minutes before the Simca showed up. The young woman behind the wheel gave me an encouraging smile as I climbed in.

She was an expert driver. No evasive action. On Sunday afternoon traffic was light, and she stuck to main thoroughfares that were wide and straight and easy to scan: Boulevard Saint-Germain, the left-bank *quais* to the Pont de la Concorde, Rue Royale. She checked her rear-view mirrors constantly. Driving up Boulevard Malesherbes, she confidently declared, "Home free."

We turned into smaller streets. In the neighborhood called Europe, she ducked down a ramp off Rue d'Ostende into an underground garage. Laurent stepped out of the shadows and got into the back seat. We drove off and soon were outside the city limits in Clichy, where we parked on a side street, Rue Alfred Locussol, in front of a row of drab low buildings. Then four flights up an unlighted stairway. A door on the highest landing opened.

Laurent's friend had let us in. There was no one else in the bare apartment. Our driver went back downstairs. We shook hands and went into a back room with four straight-backed chairs and a plain wooden table. On it were three stacks of papers and an open black imitation-leather briefcase. We sat down.

The officer was wearing gabardine slacks, an old gray polo shirt, and black loafers. He was pleasant-looking, early-fortyish, a little plump for his age. He wasted no time.

"Monsieur Mathews, it seems you have no suspicion of your predicament." I said that I'd done nothing that could get me into a "predicament." He stopped me from explaining. "We know your story. Believe me, it's irrelevant now. I'm talking to you because the situation is serious and Laurent is an old friend. What I am doing contravenes normal practice, to say nothing of regulations."

I was, I said, immensely grateful to him. "But doesn't *your* story depend entirely on the word of one Israeli agent?"

He raised his eyebrows. Laurent said, "I let that slip."

"No, it doesn't. In any case, we know this woman – *I* know her. She's reliable, tough, and nobody's fool. We have collected items that corroborate her information."

"All right. So what makes my predicament so serious?"

"Let's say the authorities of my country wouldn't want you done away with on French soil. That's the main reason for my presence here. We did not imagine that you could remain so profoundly unaware of what was happening. Not even Laurent's warnings seemed to frighten you. I decided I'd better spell things out before it was too late. Of course, it may already be too late."

I thought: this sounds like a movie I'd rather watch than be in.

"Laurent, would you mind stepping into the next room? You are not to become implicated any further, understood? And Monsieur Mathews, you must keep Georges Perec out of this from now on."

"He's my best . . . OK."

Laurent left. The man from S.D.E.C.E. looked at me the way a math teacher looks at a pupil who will never master the rule of three. He spoke to me slowly and quietly.

"We do not know which individual or individuals killed Christa Knemius last April. We are sure, however, that whoever it was belonged to, or at least was hired by, Italian neo-fascist groups working in collaboration with their French counterparts. Now the Baader-Meinhof people, and their friends on both sides of the Iron Curtain, are not the kind to take the assassination of one of their own lying down. In previous cases they have attempted and sometimes succeeded in taking a 'just' revenge on those they thought responsible. It is no different this time. They want to see Christa Knemius's murderer eliminated. And since her death, right-wing elements in this country have been feeding radical-left circles with evidence that points to you. Photographs, for example – "

"Photographs?"

"One shows you being warmly greeted by Riccardo Collantonio in the Galleria in Milan – Collantonio is a renegade member of the MSI who was almost certainly involved in the Knemius bombing. In another you are in the church of Saint Sulpice retrieving a packet deposited by one of Ordre Nouveau's *gros bras* (there's a picture of him, too). You can also be seen dining at a hotel in Graz that Hubert Massol happened to be visiting. Didn't that name mean anything to you?"

"He kidnapped Pétain's coffin. I found that out afterwards."

"Another well-known right-winger. There is a photograph of you being expelled from a meeting of the French Communist Party for distributing subversive information."

"Did you get that from a man who calls himself a Trotskyite – a Lambertiste?"

"You know perfectly well I can't answer questions like that. Then there's a photograph of you consorting with one of Le Pen's bodyguards at a soirée in Moret-sur-Loing. Of you at a dinner at Ferdinand Zendol's – Monsieur Mathews, what in God's name were you doing there? The man's a dangerous lunatic. Most recently of you and Holeindre, who happens to be security boss in Le Pen's new party. I have them right here in case – "

"I believe you. The meetings happened all right. I didn't know who any of those people were. And I actually got into Zendol's house by sheer accident." The officer made no comment. "How come you have the photographs?"

"We have reliable informants. That's how we know what these people are up to."

"And you let them commit murder?"

"Why do you think I'm here? One fact you must remember: we are not law-enforcement officers. Our job is to find out what's going on. Period. We only pass along information to magistrates and the police when national security is at stake. You hardly qualify."

"I guess I'm really lucky."

He ignored my remark. "We also have copies of highly compromising letters typed by you on Locus Solus stationery. We have tapes of telephone conversations between you and right-wing activists. Obviously" – he raised a hand to fend off my protest – "obviously all doctored material. But someone who wants to be convinced won't notice.

"Present circumstances are also against you. What has just happened in Chile is generally condemned. Whatever its true role, most people assume CIA helped overthrow Allende. Your reputation as an American agent, which you have gone to such lengths to consolidate, means that you will find little sympathy in the excitable world of 'informed' opinion – what we call *le parisianisme.*

"Finally, the rumor is being spread that your 'business' in Lans-en-Vercors – the intelligence cover you rather cleverly established – disguises other disreputable activities. It always astonishes me that making sexual innuendoes about someone already under suspicion never fails to discredit him further, no matter how his critics themselves may behave. Your withdrawals to the mountains under the pretence of writing and skiing and running your little company are seen as occasions for orgies of singular 'kinkiness,' isn't that your word? After all, what else is there to do in a dump like Lans-en-Vercors?"

"If only it were true. But can't the photographs and tapes be shown up as fakes?"

"What you forget is that the people you should be worrying about are longing to find a scapegoat. A picture may be worth a thousand words, but it's the caption that decides *which* thousand words. The simplest explanation of frequenting fascist terrorists is complicity."

"What's going to happen?"

"First, two facts. You have been recruited by fascist organisations as their agent, whether you like it or not – 'willy-nilly,' as you say. A counterintelligence maxim then applies: there is no way to unrecruit an agent. That is the first fact. The second is that no one is going to help you out of this fix."

I asked if he could tell me anything about Patrick.

"My dear sir, are you quite blind? Our organisation can do no more than what I'm doing now. I've already discreetly contacted your people. They wash their hands of you. Why? Because they offered to integrate your Locus Solus gambit and you turned them down. I quote one of them (I believe his code name is Bud): 'A great opportunity for a dangle operation, and instead he goes homesteading. Tough shit.' You are going to have to look out for yourself."

"And that means?"

"Much of the 'evidence' I have referred to was delivered by various means to extremist members of the German left. Your elimination has been authorized. Fortunately, the original timetable has not been strictly followed. You should in fact have been definitively removed from our society no later than yesterday. This information, I assure you, only reached me during the last twenty-four hours.

"A week ago a thirty-year-old East German male swam the final miles of the Oder into the Baltic Sea. As he had planned, he was picked up in the estuary by a Swedish freighter that was sailing for Hamburg. There he was successfully able to claim asylum as a political refugee, a status supported by false papers, a good briefing, and his apparently desperate means of escape. This man is a professional killer on loan from Stasi at the request of either the Baader-Meinhof group or someone representing it. My private opinion is that his fee will ultimately be paid by those who killed Christa Knemius in Milan. Incidentally, one report has it that he was once her lover; I am skeptical about that.

"He should have arrived in Paris Friday. Luckily for you, in Hamburg he went to a party where he consumed an excessive quantity of so-called Indian millet cakes – as you may know, they contain a powerful hallucinogen. (I've never tried them myself, but they are apparently – *comment dites-vous ?* – 'something else.') Your assassin needed a long rest.

"He is no longer resting. You must waste no time disappearing from the face of the earth. Before someone else helps you do just that. *Monsieur Mathews, vous êtes dans des sales draps.*"

He rose and waved me towards the door.

"Laurent – ?"

"Perhaps you will meet again another day. Francine is waiting downstairs. She will drive you wherever you need to go. *Bonne chance, Monsieur.*"

Francine found a place to park around the corner from my apartment. She said she'd wait as long as I wanted – I had time to spare before catching the 7 p.m. train to Grenoble. At home I collected my necessities: driver's licenses, passport, checkbooks, credit card, and address book, adding outstanding bills and unanswered letters, a couple of books, a box of cigars, and a long-bladed kitchen knife. They all fitted easily into a small shoulder bag. I had everything else I needed in Lans.

I was going through the papers in my desk drawer when I saw Marie-Claude's envelope. Patrick and Laurent had succeeded in putting it right out of my mind. It contained a single airplane ticket, Alitalia one-way to Venice, departure late Friday afternoon. A note attached read: "For the love of God use it. I'll miss you."

Checking my files, I found a few carbons of letters I'd never written; I didn't even try to guess who'd put them there. They were soon stuffed in a shopping bag with all my Locus Solus stationery. Francine agreed to dispose of it.

She dropped me two blocks from Gare de Lyon. I got onto my train as it was about to leave and bought my ticket on board. A vendor supplied a sandwich and beer. There weren't many people around at the Grenoble station when I arrived a little after midnight. I took a taxi to Lans and, since there wasn't another car in sight, on to the hamlet below my house. I walked up the hill the rest of the way and was home by 1 a.m.

I stole into the house and listened: not a sound. The windows were all shuttered, but I left the lights off. I knew my way over every inch of the place. I took a flashlight upstairs with me, just in case. In my bedroom I listened some more; nothing. I opened the door to the bathroom and walked through to a kind of corridor where I'd installed closets and shelves. While I was undressing I heard a familiar sound overhead: dormice playing with their stolen walnuts. They could go on playing till it was sleep-time this year. I wouldn't be bothering them.

The dormice weren't playing their usual soccer game. The walnuts were being dropped, not rolled. They were being dropped at regular, slowly lengthening intervals of a second or two. Then the sound stopped. I went out into the studio and climbed to the attic level. The attic door was open, which meant that someone had been here, or was still here. I thought of going back for the kitchen knife – I was half-naked, with only a flashlight. I turned it on and walked in.

I immediately noticed something unfamiliar amid all the junk. For fifteen years I'd saved the mechanism of a grandfather clock that I'd found in the house when I bought it. It had now been set on top of an upended steamer trunk, high enough to keep the pendulum weight a foot off the floor. Lying underneath it was a small transparent plastic bag with two walnuts inside; it was attached to the pendulum by fine cooking string.

Another strand of coarse twine was knotted to the pendulum shaft. This led out the attic door and down (I later discovered) under the granary door through the bathroom to the door from the bedroom. The far end of the twine had been looped around a piece of cardboard wedged under the door to secure the twine. My opening the door had knocked the twine free; and this in turn had released the pendulum, which it had been holding off-center. The pendulum had started swinging back and forth, raising and lowering the bag of walnuts at each swing until the bag's drag and weight brought it to a stop. That had given me time enough to hear it.

Maybe I was about to be blown to kingdom come; maybe not. I picked up the plastic bag and shined the flashlight on it. Inside, along with the walnuts, was a piece of paper folded in eight. I spread the paper out on the floor:

> I am hoping you hear this awake! No time for relax. They know you are here. The murder come Monday noontime. Already others come. Listen to messages! After burn up tape.
>
> Not use phone. Go now – soonest now best.
>
> I wish all continued in the same mode as so far. If you are alive, think kind ways of Mossad girls.
>
> You ask – I ask! – why at all do I enter projects of this sort? O, Mundorys Lorsea, I am in love with your books.
>
> Your Friend Yana Marr
>
> This go in toilet!

Mundorys Lorsea and Yana Marr were names from my novels.

I was scared enough to appreciate Yana's advice; but I couldn't follow it. If I was going to disappear, I needed money. The simplest way to get it was to take out the two thousand dollars I had deposited at a local bank when it opened next morning. If I left now, I'd have to stop at other branches of the bank, drawing only the two hundred dollar limit each time. And this meant stopping in towns, which I hoped to avoid as long as I could.

I also longed for a little sleep. I'd leave in the morning. In the kitchen I felt out a bottle of wine in the corner rack, found a corkscrew and a tumbler, and drank half the bottle before setting my alarm clock and sliding into bed.

I WOKE UP AT SIX, AFTER FOUR RESTLESS HOURS. THE CLOSET corridor had a glass-brick ceiling, and this let in enough daylight from the studio for me to pack by. I started filling my largest knapsack: toilet articles, change of shirt and underwear, blanket, a book, maps, flashlight, matches, compass, canteen, windbreaker, sweater, toilet paper, dark glasses, second jackknife with corkscrew, binoculars, writing materials, extra socks. There was still room for the food I'd buy later. I set out my clothes for the day: corduroy trousers and waistcoat, flannel shirt, thin silk socks to wear under thick wool ones, hiking boots, soft felt hat. I took a bath and shaved, then got dressed. I listened to the tape on the answering machine until I heard Marie-Claude Quintelpreaux's voice, then tore it out of its cassette and burned it together with "Yana's" note. On my way out I picked up two skipoles to use as walking sticks.

I left the house by a window at the back of the garage and started down the hill under cover of woods. A welcome early-morning fog was carpeting the valley floor. Autumn had arrived without my realizing it.

I felt pretty sure I'd gone unnoticed on my way through the hamlet, along the new development by the marshes, and past the last houses of the village. I arrived at the intersection of the Lans-Autrans road and the highway from Grenoble. Across the intersection was a small gas station with café attached.

The place was run by a friendly couple, Jean-Claude and Mireille Jallifier. They were surprised to see me – I wasn't the kind to be up this early. I said I wanted to get started on a long day's hike – I specified, "in the Chartreuse," where I had no intention of going. I had bread with butter and raspberry jam and café au lait.

On the counter phone I called Loulou, who was not only my caretaker but a good friend. I didn't call him by name. I asked if he had time to give me a lift – a pretty long one. He said he did. Then he should pick me up at 8 at the old trolley stop between the intersection and the Lans town square.

Jean-Claude said, "Someone was asking about you yesterday. A great big guy. He's down here to go hare-shooting."

"What did you tell him?"

"We said we thought you weren't here."

"I arrived last night. He was French?"

"As Parisian as they come."

Loulou picked me up as planned. Could he spare me a couple of hours? I had problems, nothing serious, but I wanted to drop out of sight for a while.

"Problems with a lady?"

"Something like that." I asked him to take me first to his apartment in Villard-de-Lans – he'd better go up and warn Jackie, his wife, that I'd be spending half an hour there. After that he could buy a few things for me: bread, cold cuts, cheese, fruit – enough for two meals.

"No wine?"

"And a bottle of red. At 9 I'll walk up to the Société Lyonnaise. Be outside the bank at 9:20 sharp. We want to leave town heading north."

I barely saw Jackie. She was taking her eldest daughter to school, with the younger daughter in tow. I asked her not to mention my visit to anyone.

I was at the bank at 9 and soon had my money. Loulou was waiting outside, two wheels on the sidewalk. At the northern edge of town, I directed him onto the bypass that would take us south.

We drove into the upper stretch of the Gorges de la Bourne. The sun slanting down its eastern slope turned it into a glory of yellowing beech. We left the Pont de la Goule Noire on our right and headed straight south into the Drôme Department and the wilder part of the Vercors. Almost no traffic: we did thirty-five twisty kilometers in just over half an hour, as far as the dirt road that led up to La Coche. That was where I planned to start walking.

The dirt road was closed: *Exploitation forestière en cours*, the sign said. That wasn't the end of the world. Five kilometers farther on, we could drive up to an alternate trail. Just before the Col de Rousset, we turned off the highway onto a paved road that wound around a hill called La Grande Serre till it ended on the Montagne de Beure.

I reminded Loulou: not a word about any of this. Unless the police got curious, which was unlikely: he should then tell them everything he knew. Right now he should go straight back to Villard, with no stops along the way. He nodded. We'd known each other for almost ten years. He wished me luck and drove off.

I packed the provisions he'd bought and took my time getting my knapsack strapped snug against my shoulders; then picked up my skipoles and turned eastward. There were numerous trails crossing the Vercors to the east; I was counting on this to win me time to make my getaway. I'd decided to follow a path over the high southernmost pastures. At the edge of the massif I'd climb down to the uninhabited valleys a couple of thousand feet below, and make my way to an isolated village called Chichiliane. From there I'd travel by local buses from one place to the next until I got "elsewhere" – I didn't know where that might be, out of the country for sure, but I expected that in a few days I'd be able to feel safe again.

For a while the trail was very wide, a good ten yards, with woods on both sides. Leaving my house, I'd noticed that there were plants still flowering: hawkweed picris, purple clover, white ox-eye, small-flowered crane's bill, hemp-nettle, vetch. Here there wasn't a flower to be seen – it was too high for that this late in the year. The beeches had all turned completely yellow; a bright dog-rose hip was the only other spot of color. The sky had been blue further north, now it was mottled pearl-gray. With thirty pounds on my back I didn't mind that. Except it meant the south wind might be rising – a bad-weather wind.

I've always found it difficult when hiking to keep futile thoughts out of my head, especially paranoid ones. It was no different today, even though I already had enough to worry about. I imagined the following scene: Georges Perec, Laurent Duchamp, his friend, and miscellaneous shills were sitting around a well-appointed table roaring with laughter. They'd organized an elaborate hoax, I'd fallen for it, and they knew they had me running across France like a doused cat. So they were laughing, and here I was starting on a long useless trek through the mountains. There may have been a little wishful thinking in my fantasy (on top of the paranoia) but it wasn't completely unreasonable, simply because I still couldn't seriously believe in the conspiracy Laurent's friend had described. Being made the victim of a practical joke seemed to me just as plausible. Of course I couldn't bring myself to accept this either, even if I wished I could (I could then go home and even back to Paris to join in the fun). And soon enough I realized that no hoax could explain away Patrick or Hubert Massol or Roger Holeindre. Or Ferdinand Zendol for that matter, even if getting involved with him had been nothing more than a coincidence.

It may have been a coincidence, but I soon found out it was no accident. I'd been walking for about half an hour and passed the refuge called the Chalet des Ours when, a quarter of a mile further on, I felt a strong urge to relieve myself. I turned a few yards off the trail into a stand of beeches that pretty well concealed me, and I was able to take off my knapsack and settle down with a semblance of privacy. I was still down on my haunches when I heard someone coming up the trail, and soon, through the curtain of yellow leaves, I was able to see who it was. It was a man; a big man; Zendol himself. He had a small army-green shoulder bag slung over his left hip; he carried a pump shotgun under his right arm. He stopped right in front of me. I thought, *Squat squat squat! Squat squat!* He took three bright red shells out of his bag and chambered them. I said to myself: no one shoots hares with a pump shotgun; no one hunts hares without a dog.

After that I stopped thinking. I didn't decide what to do. What happened happened as if it was programmed and I'd become a word in someone else's grammar. I watched Zendol slip the safety off and start up the trail. He was intently on the lookout for something ahead of him. I fastened my pants belt and picked up a skipole. I stepped onto the trail, I heard an unearthly voice shout, "Athena, guide my arm!" and ran at Zendol so fast he didn't have time to turn around before I'd struck the back of his neck with the tip of the skipole. Athena had been listening: the point hit the spot where the spine meets the base of the skull. Zendol's arms snapped out sideways; he fell forwards like a toppled tree. I stood over him: he lay still. I didn't bother to check for vital signs.

The bag had fallen off his shoulder; he'd dropped his gun. I picked him up by the feet and dragged him off the downhill side of the trail into a clump of birch and red pine. Beyond the trees the ground tumbled down towards the Drôme River. I took his wallet and all his papers: passport, ID card, driver's license, hunting license, credit cards, plane ticket, checkbook, a letter from his mother. I swung his gun and bag over the slope beyond him and watched them roll out of sight. I found myself richer by six thousand two hundred and fifteen francs.

I reattached my knapsack, collected my skipoles, and started walking again. I didn't feel anything much about what I'd done.

I didn't know what to feel. In my whole adult life I'd only once struck a man in anger. There was some anger now, but after the fact of course, and of the speculative kind: because I understood why Zendol had come after me. His gang wanted to make sure I was killed. Christa Knemius's murderer would be accounted for, and they could blame the leftists for what had happened to me. They might even get the East German hired gun arrested – two birds with one stone. They were people one should definitely avoid.

It wasn't likely that Zendol had come here to shoot hares, was it?

I found myself walking on solid rock, the top of the limestone mass that lies under the sticky red soil. Soon I came into summer pasturage – miles of it, no trees, nothing but cropped grass mixed with a familiar low-growing plant: years before I'd dug up a sample on some other mountain and planted it in my yard. Its name is alpine lady's mantle; it's as lovely as its name, with small delicately-toothed silver-edged round leaves. Nothing but green everywhere, except for a tiny spot of burning blue, a flowering alpine gentian, *Gentiana nivalis*, somehow spared by the ewes' efficient jaws.

Just short of its highest point my path joined a major trail, GR 93. (GR stood for *sentier de Grande Randonnée*, or "main hiking trail.") I was supposed to follow it for several miles. I saw a man sitting on the top of the rise to the left of the path, but he turned out to be the silhouette of two adjacent cairns. He frightened me more than Zendol had.

A real man was approaching in the opposite direction. No gun. We spent a few minutes talking. He was from Grane, in the Drôme valley. We compared local restaurants, and I realized I hadn't eaten anything since breakfast. I told him where I was heading (not mentioning Chichiliane) and he gave me a few pointers. He warned me about the weather up there, how it could turn nasty in the space of a few minutes.

After he'd gone, I sat down and ate. A little bread, meat, and cheese, some wine, a pint of water, a few green grapes. I felt better, a lot surer of what I was doing. I fell into a nice walking rhythm. Up and down, up and down – I stopped paying attention to the landscape except when I emerged from the occasional patch of woods. The Grand Veymont, the highest peak in the Vercors, got steadily closer in the northeast. I passed the shepherd's refuge at Pré-Peyret and waved to a man tending a flock a hundred yards below. The junction with GR 91 happened on schedule. I turned right, and twenty minutes later right again on what I took to be the way to the ancient Roman quarry – the way to Chichiliane.

I WALKED ALONG LEVEL GROUND FOR A WHILE. THAT WAS WHAT my map indicated – it was a large-scale map put out by the Geographical Institute. I went along, happy in my confident, easygoing stride, any worry I might have had allayed by the red and white stones that appeared periodically and identified the trail as a GR. The trouble was, the trail I should have been on was *not* a GR, and I didn't realize this until I found myself staring at the Montagne de Glandasse. I checked the map: I'd come too far south.

I saw where I'd made my mistake. I'd already lost an hour, and it was after five o'clock before I got back to the wrong turning. Twilight was only two hours away.

There was a little ridge above the place where the two trails met, and I climbed onto it with my binoculars to survey the ground I'd covered that afternoon. I had no trouble making out my trail, and I followed it back until I saw what I was dreading. About three miles away a man was moving along the trail in my direction. He was moving fast; he must be traveling light. His hair was bright blond. Or I imagined it was.

I started out on the trail east, the trail I'd missed, walking as quickly as I could, which wasn't very quick. I was feeling tired for the first time. I told myself that fear can do that and it wasn't real physical fatigue. And so what? I was frightened. I wasn't frightened of dying (I couldn't even conceive of it) but of being humiliated – being caught and cornered because I'd been so dumb. I tried comforting myself with the thought that the man behind me might not be pursuing me at all, and that even if he was, he might take the same wrong path I had; but my remorse was too great for me to believe that. When I made an effort to walk faster, I began tripping over the uneven rock. Because of the cloud cover it was getting dark earlier than I expected. I remembered once at this time of year, and this time of day, walking down through woods to my house in Lans. The last sunlight was shining horizontally through a succession of beech branches in every stage of changing color – green, green-yellow, golden-yellow, russet. I'd thought: a hymn to mutability. Here there was no mutability or sun or trees. Gray cliff on my left, gray earth on my right, gray rock under my feet.

Soon I couldn't see the ground in front of me clearly any more. The trail was straight, which meant a flashlight beam could be seen hundreds of yards back. But then I fell, twice, and I knew I had no choice. I strapped one skipole to the back of my knapsack and pulled out my flashlight from one of its side pockets. I held it pointed low in front of me. The going was slower, I was getting seriously discouraged and kept pushing ahead because there was nothing else to do. I'd stop every so often and look behind me: silence, darkness getting darker.

About an hour into the night something happened that changed things. I'm not sure what it was – maybe a wobbly stone threw me off balance, or I caught my foot in a crevice, or I tripped over my own feet. I fell, hard, to my right. I knew the cliff was on my left, but to the right I couldn't see anything, and there wasn't anything. I was briefly airborne. I hit a steep slope and bounced down it. A branch caught me in the ribs and knocked the wind out of me. I banged my left temple against a stone and yelled silently, with no sensation outside that stunning pain.

A scratchy whipping effect meant shrubs were slowing me down. I rolled onto soft earth. Flashlight and knapsack were gone. I was alone in the absolute dark. What else could I do but hold my bleeding head and lie still?

Stopping at the sheer edge will never abolish space.

On these high plateaux summers are far apart. Autumn snows cover them early, and visible life deserts them. Come October, and flocks and their shepherds are gone. Killing frosts turn the grasses to blackening brown, and increasingly frequent snow-showers blanket them deeper and deeper. Sometimes the south wind turns warm enough to soften the upper inches of what has fallen before: after a night or two, the slush freezes; thus alternating layers of snow and ice are built up to a height of many feet. North winds and south winds sweep over an expanse of white desolation broken only by jutting rocks with sides too sheer for the snow to settle on. Months pass before the days grow long enough and the sun grows warm enough, late in the spring season, for the snow cover first to sink and then break apart, baring streaks and fuzzy patches of grizzled muddied earth; and still more weeks go by before the residual grass starts turning green and the first small birds return.

I HUDDLED IN MY SMALL DARK PLACE, HUGGING MYSELF. I KEPT my eyes tight shut.

A dreary hymn from schooldays had started moaning its way through my brain.

> *New every morning is the love*
> *Our wakening and uprising prove*

– I thought: *pruv.* We used to sing in a bewildered drone. "Uprising" came out "apprising."

> *The trivial round the common task*
> *Will furnish all we need to ask*

I'd vaguely wondered, what's a trivial? How do you wrap a task in it? And the common task – going to the bathroom, maybe? After every breakfast I'd be asked, "Did you do your duty?" A potty. Shit.

> *Room to deny ourselves a road*
> *To bring us daily nearer God*

(*God* pronounced *goad*?) Why would anyone want to do that? Shouldn't we be trying to get on that road instead of denying it? When I asked my dutiful mother, did she believe in Goad? she'd say, only as a *force.* Goad is a force. Force drives blood through skin of golden pear on its tree. Drives bilge through sick intestines in oceanic surge. Toughens penis driving into girl's dry vulva while other soldier rubs cock waiting his turn. Drives blast out of gun inside prisoner's mouth, now his tongue is hanging out the back of his head, the pear on the tree is stippled.

> *New treasures still of countless price*
> *God will provide for sacrifice*

I didn't get it. I didn't care.

I stretched out face down. I was lying on something else – oilskin. I rolled onto my back: dark, but less so. A coarse wool blanket covered me, head included. Around me fidgety sounds. I pulled down the blanket and saw a small amount of blue sky through a ring of slit snouts, little eyes peering down at me out of woolly heads with perked-up ears. I started to sit up, the sheep quietly backed away. I turned onto my knees and pushed myself up. The blood pulsed in the places where I'd hurt myself, my head resolutely banging away.

I was on a slanting pasture, next to the slope I'd fallen down: it looked only twenty feet high, apparently enough to knock the stuffing out of me. The sun was still behind the mountains. There was a dusting of snow over everything, melting already. The sheep had gone back to grazing. I wobbled a few steps and pissed into the slope.

A male voice called out, not far off. I watched the man coming towards me: short, slender, dressed in jeans and a dirty hip-length windbreaker. He wore absurdly small plain shoes and carried a long cane. Six feet away he stopped. He hadn't shaved in several days, but his mustache still looked cheerful. Brown, lively eyes, a little wary.

"You OK?"

I nodded. "And this – ?" I asked, pointing to the poncho and blanket.

"I couldn't wake you up. You'd grunt and roll away. That was about two hours ago. It started snowing. You haven't got a fever?"

"No, I just hurt. I fell – "

"We'll talk about it later. You see the refuge down a ways? My fiancée's there. Can you make it on your own? I don't like leaving my babies unless I have to." *Mes petits*, he called them. "Chantal will take care of you."

He'd rounded up my knapsack and skipoles. Handing me the poles, he said he'd bring the sack down later. I started to thank him. *"C'est tout naturel."*

"My name's Harry."

"Jean-Marie."

We shook hands. He pointed to a far corner of the field. I followed the sheep tracks to the refuge.

Chantal had me spotted long before I got to their front door – the only door. She clasped her hands to her heart as I came closer. She wasn't exactly what the word fiancée suggested: a kindly-looking, middle-aged woman in a flower-print smock and the checked rubber-soled house slippers called *charentaises*, her graying hair tied back in a blue kerchief.

"Good Lord! Come in here right away." I knew my clothes were a mess, but it was my head that worried her. She sat me down and filled a bowl from a kettle steaming on the wood-burning stove. She fetched a clean dishtowel and soaked and wrung out one end of it, then started bathing my temple and neck. Each time she rinsed the towel the water got redder. Finally she patted me dry and unhooked a small mirror that she held in front of me: I saw an open gash across the swelling. She found some hydrogen peroxide and tamped the cut and finally taped a compress over it. "*Merde!* I didn't wash my hands." I felt like hugging her.

"Some bread and coffee? Or maybe sausage and a glass of wine?" Bread and coffee, I said. She put a jar of honey on the table by the bread. "Your name's Harry?" I realized I'd better start paying attention. "Someone left a package for you earlier. She was sure you'd be along."

"I don't even know where I am."

"On the Peyre Rouge. A very young woman, a foreigner, she didn't speak much French. She had no left hand – you don't see who I mean? She was all right, I can tell you that." I told Chantal it wasn't anyone I knew. "We had another visit yesterday evening. Are you American? He asked if we'd seen an American hiker. He was a young foreigner, too, but not all right, not one bit, barging in and asking his questions and taking off without another word. *Un sale Fritz*. We've seen enough of them in our time."

There was a note in the envelope. I knew the handwriting from the walnut machine in my house – "Yana Marr."

> In immediacy danger is removed. Still take continuous care in months that come. I am a little proud.
>
> I know so much more about you than you know. I feel so much more than you feel.
>
> There is enclosed a souvenir.
>
> I sign myself:
>
> Georges's fathers' mother (Judah's signifying other)

I'd figure out the "signature" some other time. The souvenir was a spent bright-red buckshot shell, like Zendol's.

Later, Jean-Marie took me aside. "There was a shot last night, around half past ten. You didn't hear it? I guess you were already out of it. I'd gotten up to check on my babies. Just one shot. Strange."

CHANTAL COOKED US BEEF STEW AND PAN-FRIES FOR LUNCH. I could see she'd been a handsome woman, and she still would have been if she hadn't spent so much of her life out of doors. To a lesser extent the same was true for Jean-Marie.

I'd told her earlier that I ought to be moving on, knowing perfectly well what she'd say: "Certainly not. Why, you may have had a concussion. You rest up today and get a good night's sleep. Then we'll see."

I asked how they managed to bring their provisions up here – the nearest road ended miles away. "Madeleine." I met Madeleine that afternoon: a stocky chestnut mare. She was tethered to a tree with a long lead that gave her plenty of grazing room. "Fifteen years old and tough as nails." Jean-Marie was looking ahead at his flock of four hundred merinos; and something caught his shepherd's eye and sent him hurrying across the field through the feeding ewes. He'd spotted trouble at eighty yards: one of his *petits* was ailing. Jean-Marie got down on his knees, ran his hand under her belly, pulled each of her eyes wide open, looked into her mouth. "She's eaten some kind of crap. She's got to be purged. Do me a favor, go back to Chantal and tell her what's wrong. She'll know what I need."

I took off at a run. When I came back with a liter bottle full of black liquid, he was sitting where I'd left him, with the ewe's head in his lap. He was rubbing her behind the ears and talking soft sheep talk. I uncorked the bottle and handed it to him, he held her head in the crook of one arm and poked the bottle deep inside her mouth – it gurgled into her for a good five seconds. The ewe didn't like it, but she put up with it. Trust was trust. He could have laid her on a rock and cut her throat, pinching her nostrils so she'd die quicker, and she would have died trusting him. He never forgot they were being raised for slaughter; but he loved his ewes.

I SPENT THE AFTERNOON TRYING TO MAKE MYSELF USEFUL. Watching the flock wasn't an option. I wouldn't know how to handle any problems, and as for keeping the ewes from straying, the sheepdogs took care of that: three lively little mongrels who were madly good at their job. Their only defect was too much enthusiasm – they didn't only bark and snap at the sheep but sometimes bit their back legs to herd them. Ten days later Jean-Marie put down my favorite bitch because she'd maimed two slow-going ewes at the back of the flock – this happened at the end of the *transhumance*, the sheepwalk that moves a flock between its summer and winter pastures.

The *transhumance* was the reason I wanted to ingratiate myself with Jean-Marie and Chantal. If I could be a part of it, I'd be safe. Sheepwalks steer clear of towns and paved roads. When they do run into traffic, no one pays any attention beyond what it takes to get clear of them. So I fetched odds and ends for Jean-Marie, split wood for the stove, tidied up any loose gear I found. I even brought Madeleine an apple from the larder, with Chantal's permission.

I don't know if my hustling made any difference, but that evening I got my wish. We'd had a supper of bean soup, smoked lard, and cheese. I felt sure Jean-Marie had consulted Chantal, and I knew she was fond of me. Jean-Marie asked: could I give them a hand for a week or so? I said nothing would suit me better. Jean-Marie wondered if I had problems. I answered, yes and no. Not with the law, anyway. A bunch of hotheads was giving me a hard time. "That's why I go walking in the mountains at night. I think they're off my back, though."

"That's what the young woman was talking about," Chantal said.

"Very good. We'll start off day after tomorrow. It's snowed already, which means a hard frost is on its way, and that's something that makes the ewes abort. They'll be lambing in a few weeks. We're taking them south, a little village in Provence called Violès, just north of Carpentras. It may take us ten days to get there. Once we're down in the valley, we'll have a car – Chantal's son and daughter are joining us. They can drive ahead and check out our route and find places where we can stop. With them along we'd manage, but we could use an extra hand. We can't pay you, but you'll eat well. Better than up here, with the car for shopping."

We toasted our partnership with another glass of red wine. Good wine, I said. Strong wine. "Violès wine," said Jean-Marie.

THE DAY WE LEFT WE WERE UP TWO HOURS BEFORE DAWN. We finished our packing and cleaned up the refuge. All of us carried hefty loads on our backs; we strapped the rest onto Madeleine. As soon as it was light we started out. Chantal led the way. Two Rovre goats followed a ways behind her, a bearded castrated buck and a milkable nanny. They had high curved horns and looked like emblems on some emperor's shield. The flock plodded after them, with Jean-Marie surveying it from the rear and the three dogs yapping up and down on either side. Last of all came Madeleine.

I was supposed to guide her, but she knew more about rocks and slopes than I would ever learn; so in fact I followed her lead, and things went fairly well until we came to a junction with a road where Jean-Marie had left his wagon. We transferred all our gear to it and hitched up Madeleine before going on. That was when she and I began turning into intimate enemies.

I didn't dislike her, and she tolerated me; but we had a problem. A red flag hung at the back of the wagon. It was a warning sign to anyone driving up from behind to slow down. The rule was that this flag had to be kept fifty yards from the tail end of the flock; and Madeleine was a sociable animal – she was a horse – and had no intention of being so far away from the sheep, dogs, and humans she knew so well. For seven hours a day she battled to catch up with them. She had weight (close to a ton), strength, and fourteen years' savvy going for her; I had reins, the bit, and my hard rubber heels, which I kept dug into the ground for most of the hundred and fifty miles we covered.

It was punishing work. But I didn't really mind: that life might have been invented for me. Being out of doors night and day made me forget I had a body to worry about. Living and working with these new friends left no room for unhappiness. There were Jean-Marie and his flock, and the rest of us shared the single goal of helping him take care of it. This was what filled up all of our days from before dawn till nightfall (and Jean-Marie got up several times during the night to inspect his petits). I felt I didn't need anything outside our world. We'd pass villages, and I'd look at the ordinary people in them, people who slept in beds and got bored with their jobs and with each other, and I felt I was a god in a world of puppets.

The trail we'd followed when we started out had brought us across the Balcon du Glandasse and down to a point just above the valley of the Meyrousse. There we found not only Madeleine's wagon waiting for us but Chantal's children and a car. They'd already rented a field for the night, between two hamlets called Les Plateaux and Les Liotards, where we could camp and the sheep could graze. I started to get to know them at supper that evening.

They'd both taken a week of their yearly vacation to help out Jean-Marie. Pierre was about thirty-five, trim, soft-spoken; he worked as a bank teller in Valence. Nathalie, who taught grade school in Grenoble, was a few years younger than her brother; petite, pretty, pert, no make-up, curly auburn hair cut short. She liked to laugh, and she was a good listener, whoever might be talking. She loved teasing her mother and Jean-Marie. She was respectful to her brother and deferred to him most of the time. As for me, she seemed to think I'd stepped straight out of a western movie.

Except for the scenery, each day was the same. Jean-Marie woke us up around 4:30. We ate breakfast while it was still dark, then washed up – we followed the valley bottoms, so we were always near a stream. We had our gear stowed and Madeleine harnessed by sunup; we had to get the most out of the short fall days. We walked till noon or so – it was slow going, barely two miles an hour – then stopped in another field that Pierre and Nathalie had located for us the night before or during the morning. We had lunch and took an hour's siesta, mainly to rest the sheep. Then we walked till twilight and another camp. The flock spread out over the field; the three dogs stood watch around them; Jean-Marie strolled here and there looking for damaged hooves and legs. (We lost two sheep on our way: one collapsed and died for no apparent reason, the other disappeared – it may have been stolen.) I led Madeleine to the stream and let her drink her fill; afterwards I tethered her nearby. Nathalie helped Chantal prepare supper on two gas camping stoves. After gathering wood and kindling a fire, Pierre and I heated a pot for shaving and bathed ourselves, up to a point: the stream waters were glacial. I shaved every day, Pierre once every two days. Jean-Marie didn't shave until the walk was safely over. I never saw him wash at all. I gathered the women bathed in the dark after washing the dinner utensils; when I offered to help I was told not to bother them. Meanwhile Jean-Marie, Pierre, and I sat drinking and talking by the fire.

Pierre and Nathalie usually bought the local paper when they went shopping. I couldn't find any reports of bodies abandoned in the southern Vercors. I would have liked to let Loulou know I was all right, but I decided to wait till we reached Violès before writing him a note. I'd ask Pierre to mail it when he went back to Valence.

I wondered where I'd go after Violès. I hadn't forgotten that Marie Chaix was living in Provence. But I knew I should get out of the country, and I remembered Marie-Claude Quintelpreaux's airplane ticket. She'd given it to me in time to be out of harm's way: she knew what was going on, and she'd sent me to Venice. So that was a possibility.

We made our way very slowly across the bottom of the Vercors; we crossed the Drôme and climbed into the Diois: Sainte Croix, Saillans, the Col de la Chaudière, Bourdeaux. Our last five days we were in Provence. It never once rained.

LATE ONE AFTERNOON WE WERE APPROACHING THE DEFILE OF Saint-Ferréol-Trente-Pas. To the left of the road lay a vast flat meadow that stretched to hills half a mile away. Nathalie was keeping me company while I hung onto Madeleine – her presence in fact calmed the mare down. Evening was coming on. The limestone outcroppings on the hills were slowly turning from cream to gold.

Far off, on the other side of the meadow, a bay horse was grazing. He heard us, or smelled us, he looked in our direction and saw Madeleine. He let out a whinny and started gently cantering towards us. When she heard him neigh, Madeleine stopped. She pulled the wagon across the road just short of the fence running along its left shoulder. She'd forgotten about Jean-Marie and the dogs and sheep. She waited. The bay came trotting up to the fence in front of her. The two horses stood facing each other, utterly silent; their nostrils flared, their tails whisked, otherwise they didn't move. I waited a couple of minutes before giving the reins a mild yank. Madeleine quietly turned back onto the road.

I laughed, but when I said, "Gulliver was so right," my voice broke ridiculously. Nathalie looked at me. A minute passed; then she said, "I never know how to pronounce that name." She started spelling Houyhnhm out loud to me. There was no rule, I replied. When we reached the next bend, the bay was still standing where we'd left him, watching us.

Someone was kneeling by my pile of blankets. It was very late in the night. "*C'est moi.*" A rustle of clothing; she slipped between the covers. She lay naked on top of me and worked fast. She had me where she wanted before I was half awake. "Go ahead. Don't hold back." There were floods of color in the darkness. A little yellow elephant was spraying me with warm extract of cappucino. Pipes sang in palace walls. A red cartridge was being plugged into the widening cleft at the base of Zendol's skull. "Stop holding back. Let go." "Yes." In a moment there was nothing, very bright nothing. She stopped my mouth with one hand. Nothing: everyone was gone. I was warm and light. It was all gone. I started sobbing. "Ssh. It's over. You got your man – you did the right thing." I opened my eyes but it was so dark I couldn't even see her teeth. "And a woman, too." She was soon gone.

III

In 1973, when I'd applied to the DAAD for a residency in Berlin, I hadn't been a serious candidate; I was mainly adding another ornament to my masquerade. (DAAD: the Deutsche Akademische Austauch Dienst, the German academic exchange service, which had a special division for artists and writers.) Almost twenty years later, friends told me I had a good chance of being accepted, so I reapplied; and in January, 1991 I landed in Berlin and settled into a roomy apartment on Schlüterstrasse in Charlottenburg.

It was a quarter of the city I liked and even knew a little: just over a year earlier, right after the Wall had come down, I'd made an exploratory visit to Berlin before submitting my candidacy. During my stay I'd been taken once to the Paris-Bar, an attractive restaurant on Kantstrasse; and after I'd finished unpacking, I decided to go there now for lunch. It was a popular meeting-place for people connected with the arts, and I knew it was not more than a twenty-minute walk from my apartment. Getting there and back would give me a chance to reconnoiter my neighborhood.

It was a gray winter day, not really cold but chilly and damp. I was surprised by the the number and size of the trees growing in many of the nearby streets, forlornly skeletal in that season but still asserting a comforting presence of nature among the dark buildings. I walked east along Mommsenstrasse to where it ends at Knesebeckstrasse, then turned left towards Savigny Platz – I remembered there were several good bookstores on or near it; and in one of them I bought an elegant little edition of Robert Walser's story, *Der Spaziergang*. I would read a few pages of it over lunch and, I hoped, start recovering some sense of the German language I'd been neglecting for the last thirty years.

Past Savigny Platz, I turned right on Kantstrasse and a few minutes later entered my restaurant. I went in feeling pleased I hadn't lost my way.

Inside, the restaurant, pleasantly dark, was humming with conversation. I was led to a corner table where I soon ordered my meal; and I was enjoying a large glass of white Bergerac when I heard my name mentioned at the table to my left. I glanced at my neighbors in a wall mirror: two middle-aged men I didn't recognize sat side by side. I opened my book and bent over it, turning away from them.

"You never told me you knew Mathews," one of them was saying.

"I didn't know him. We were both in Paris in the late '60s."

"I'd like to meet him. He writes some pretty weird stuff. But from what I've heard, he himself is not weird."

"He was weird."

"Is it true he's CIA?"

"Not to listen to him talk. He used to bore people to death 'explaining' his reputation. Misrepresented by a well-meaning friend in Laos. I think it was Laos."

"So?"

"Oh, that was bullshit. I know he was CIA. That wasn't really the problem – lots of people are CIA. He was also a space cadet. He did oddball things that made it risky for everybody involved. Zendol told me about it. Of course Zendol was biased – I mean Mathews attacked him *physically*."

"So what happened?"

“They had to get rid of him. In fact, they took executive action.”

“Executive action?”

“He was ‘terminated with extreme prejudice’ – the wet solution.”

I had heard enough. There was not the slightest doubt that this man was telling the truth.

New York, October 25, 2003

SELECTED DALKEY ARCHIVE PAPERBACKS